Another I,
Another You

A NOVEL

Richard Schickel

HARPER & ROW, PUBLISHERS

NEW YORK, HAGERSTOWN, SAN FRANCISCO, LONDON

Portions of this work originally appeared in *Redbook*.

FIRST EDITION

Designed by Lydia Link

Library of Congress Cataloging in Publication Data

Schickel, Richard.
  Another I, another you.
  I. Title.
PZ4.S3276An 1978 [PS3569.C4846]   813'.5'4   77–3805
ISBN 0–06–013794–0

78 79 80 81 82 10 9 8 7 6 5 4 3 2 1

For all the friends of this passage,
with love and gratitude

For every news
Means pairing off in twos and twos
Another I, another you.

W. H. AUDEN

AUTHOR'S NOTE

I am not I; she is not she; they are not they.

One

"Take the flowered one."

For some reason, I recognized her voice before I turned. "Can't even go shopping anymore without people bothering you. Hi, Libby."

She was—is—a tall and slender woman: dark hair, dark complexion, yellow-brown eyes. Her nose is really too long for her face, so people always call her handsome rather than beautiful—one of those fine distinctions people not in the habit of making fine distinctions like to make, and which are useless.

We reached out for each other—the old-friends embrace. Lips brushed cheeks, dryly. Then she stepped back, caught my hands and held them firmly. She did not quickly let go. Her gaze was direct, appraising, her smile almost a grin.

"Eventually everybody comes to Bloomingdale's." I caught the reference to *Casablanca*. It was something the four of us had always done—worked old movie lines into the conversation. Often they *were* the conversation.

"Somebody's birthday," I said.

"Some somebody. Designer scarves."

"My new image. International producer. As long as the credit holds out. You look marvelous."

"So do you."

"New image. New life. Maybe it agrees with me. How do things march with you?"

Her eyes wavered slightly. When she replied, her voice was not quite so crisp. "Actually, pretty good. Now."

"Yeah. I heard about you and Hilton."

"And you and Marion?"

"Her lawyer wears white-on-white shirts and talks in a whisper like Don Corleone. He thinks he's tough."

"Maybe I should hire him."

"Maybe I should buy you a drink."

"Maybe you should, but not now. I have to get back to the office."

"Office?"

"A bunch of industrial designers. Right around the corner. We're working late tonight."

"That's right. I forgot. You were into photography." I tried to put quotation marks around that "into" as I spoke.

"Yes. But down here I'm just the gal Friday. It's dumb time. But do call. I'll even let you buy me dinner."

"Hang on a sec. I'll take the flowered one and walk you out."

"Haven't got the time. Besides, I might see another guy with a cute ass and follow him."

"Why, Elizabeth . . ."

"Don't worry. I love you for your mind, too."

She turned, making a little gesture—half wave, half salute —and strode away down the aisle.

I watched her go, all the way to the escalator. I remembered her stride. The Adderleys had lived just around the corner and from my study window I had observed their comings and goings—especially Libby's. Even burdened with groceries or being tugged along by Max, their fashionably shaggy sheepdog, there was something admirable about the way she moved, a firmness and purpose about her that set her apart. Of course, long-legged women have always attracted me.

I turned back to the counter and completed my purchase. Despite the excellent lady for whom the scarf was intended, I knew I would call her. Libby. Elizabeth. Mrs. Hilton Adderley III. The neighbor lady.

Two

At the time we met, Elizabeth and I, I was six months separated from my wife of fifteen years. Separated in the physical sense, that is. Emotionally, of course, I was still attached to her, as she was to me, I think, though she often did a better imitation of a liberated individual than I did. People were fond of telling me that it would take at least two years "for the scars to heal." Naturally, I resisted this glum view of my immediate future, though I see now it was merely one of those sayings that combine banality of expression with common wisdom in a peculiarly annoying way.

I was then in the process of doing everything everyone does to reassure himself that despite the disaster suffered by his self-esteem, despite the disruption of those habits and routines which—more than we can ever know until they suddenly evaporate—sustain us in this fragmented, fragmenting age, he is alive and functioning, capable of loving and being loved. And worthy of it.

The scarf, for instance. It was intended for a lady named Ellen MacIntyre, herself a five-year veteran of a divorce, and most wise and dear. We had known each other, circling circumspectly around one another, for a year before I had left home, and she was one of the first people I'd called for a "date" (strange, culturally laggard term) after I moved out. Within a couple of weeks we had established (currently approved term coming up) "a relationship." It was very nice. She was small and blond and quick. I loved her apartment. With its brightly flowered couches and its scattering of antiques, it was both very feminine and very stable in atmosphere. Someone who knew who she was lived here, and since I no longer possessed that information regarding myself, it was very inviting—even seductive.

Too much so. Immediately it began, I started trying to wriggle out of the relationship. I kept telling Ellen I was too self-absorbed, too mean and crazy for her. That she was too good, too patient, kind and decent for the likes of me. All of which was probably true, but did not take into account my several good points. "Why don't you learn to take yes for an answer?" she said one time, and of course, she was right. We shared tastes and interests (the ballet, tennis, Evelyn Waugh), and even a profession (she was a journalist and I had been). But I was immediately restive. I was not ready for such comfort, for the commitment she never demanded, but which I knew she needed and was ready for. I required confusions, comings and goings, even a certain mysteriousness. "They seek him here, they seek him there . . . that damned elusive Pimpernel."

Yes, I know. There's something wrong here. If you have read those commonsensical survival guides for the divorced which now proliferate in the bookshops, you know that the order of events is incorrect, that what the suddenly freed male is supposed to do is experiment widely and wildly in the first months of his freedom and then, finding these brief encounters unsatisfying, settle down with someone like Ellen for the long pull. Another long pull—all the way to the grave this time.

The thing is, I never seem to do things in the same order that other people do. Doubtless I have a contrary nature. In this particular instance, however, it is probably fair to say that

5

when I was forced out of my marriage by a wife who had grown implacably angry with me and with the life we had built (tacked together is a better phrase, madly improvised amidst the high, shifting winds of circumstance), I was in no condition to play the singles scene. For the years preceding the final split had been increasingly frigid ones, during which I had been told, occasionally by blunt statement, more often by reiterated implication, that I was a bad, perhaps hopeless, lover—unromantic by nature, too realistic in attitude, physically a klutz. I had my own unpleasant bill of particulars to throw back at Marion during these scenes, but there is no point at this late date in trying to affix percentages of guilt for the rancorous chill that grew up between us in the last years of our marriage. Suffice it to say, in the phrase of the shrink to whom we repaired seeking repair, we created between us "a climate of starvation." I don't know what aftereffects it had on Marion. We've never discussed the matter and now, having drifted into that vaguely affectionate neutrality which distinguishes the happily divorced, never will. But I had been badly hurt, was desperately insecure about my ability not just to please a woman, but even to attract her in the first place.

Ellen healed me. She had conceived for some reason a genuine admiration for me during the time we had been but casual acquaintances, and so, when I finally nerved myself to make a pass at her, she gave herself to me with an eagerness that surprised me, a tenderness I had not known in many years, a sweet gentleness that, over a period of months, restored my self-esteem, made me feel, even, a helluva fella.

Men! If they're not worried sick with fantasies of impotence, they're flying their cocks as if they were the banners of a victorious army marching rapaciously through a conquered province. Sexually we are all perpetual adolescents, and my "success" with Ellen (far better say her success with me) sent me flying through the streets in search of further prey.

I affect a certain irony here. But I am not proud of the next months. Beth. Jill. Stephanie. Wendy. Caroline. Meg. Helene.

They were all, with perhaps one unimportant exception, unfailingly kind, pleasant, sweet, patient. Some of them a sensible man would have paused with, perhaps found whatever it was he thought he was looking for. And I have very few excuses. There were, of course, those guides to reasonable divorce, which assured me that I was going through a familiar, perhaps inevitable, phase, one that most men in my circumstances experience, and that it would soon pass. I also consoled myself with the thought that my professional life, though highly profitable at that moment, was also highly unstable, with productions under way simultaneously in New York, London and Los Angeles. Bopping from one to another, I told myself, there was no practical hope of establishing a lasting relationship with any of these women, that indeed it would be unfair to them, to myself, to try to force matters beyond what appeared to be their natural level, which was cool and casual. And besides, during the decade and a half during which I had been sequestered in a faithful marriage, this sexual revolution which I had only read about (and assumed to be a media hype, as imaginary as all the other sociological phenomena the newsmagazines and networks create out of a rag, a bone and a hank of rumor) had really happened. Practically speaking, it means merely that younger women are now inclined to dispense with the traditional preliminaries of courtship, the old ritual of chaste dinners followed by hand-wrestling on the couch, the whole interspersed with earnest moral discussions, and to proceed—assuming a degree of mutual attraction—more or less directly to the bedroom. This does not mean that they are any freer than their older sisters of those behavioral enigmas that inhibit their pleasure in what ensues. Some are, and some aren't—in roughly the same ratio as pertained in the fifties. It's just that now everyone is a much better sport about the whole thing. Much of the melodrama has been drained from sex. And with it, it occurred to me, much of the romance, too.

But it would have been foolish of me, of anyone, not to take advantage of this new order. It would have required, indeed, a saintliness I do not command. And yet, quickly skilled as I became in the art of seduction, I was never entirely comfortable in the role of cocksman. For I was—I am—a true child of the fifties, and there remained some part of me that disapproved of what I was doing. I had been raised to believe— even in my youthful state of perpetual horniness—that the act of sex should be an expression of the state of love, and I still believed it. It did not stay my restlessness. It did not interfere with my performance. It just nagged at me—a moral low-back pain.

But set all talk of morality aside. What I was really missing, first in my near-domesticity with Ellen (who had very sensibly freed me to pursue my irresistible urges, while yet retaining a claim on me), then in these other affairs, was intensity of feeling. What I wanted, what I knew I needed, was—I hesitate to write it, so inappropriate does the word seem in the context of our times—a passion, something that would blot out, burn out, all sense of obligation to profession, to family, to respectability.

I had known that feeling once. I think we all have—in adolescence. When it is entirely inappropriate. The puzzled scorn of young middle-class women subjected to it had tamed me, as it used to most young men, teaching us to ration our emotions lest we appear foolish—even demented—in eyes already learning to make nice calculations regarding the long pull.

But now free of a sudden, and as one of the film editors who worked for me succinctly put it, "single, solvent and straight," that is to say eligible, I wished—wished desperately—to banish my lifelong habits of caution and circumspection, to fling myself heedlessly upon some woman and find, of course, an answering heedlessness. The world well lost.

Three

Did it occur to me, after that first meeting in the department store, that Libby Adderley was somehow the perfect, the inevitable, object for these unfulfilled romantic longings? Of course not. I'm cursed with self-consciousness, but not to that degree.

She was what she had always been—an extremely attractive woman, a friend of almost twenty years' standing who had, naturally, drifted pleasantly through my fantasy life at various times during that period. Now, suddenly, she was free and I was free and there was no reason not to see what we might find in each other (maybe much, maybe little) by confronting one another unencumbered by spouses, children, mutual friends—all the stuff that had in the past prevented us from exchanging anything like an intimate word.

I imagined, needless to say, an affair. And in imagining it I certainly took into account that slight taste of . . . danger? no, too strong a word; adventure would be more like it . . . that would surely flavor our meetings. With so much history in common, so many friends, we would, if discovered, create a small, scandalous *frisson* in certain quarters. Avoiding that would require discretion. And that, I fancied, would add a certain piquancy to our meetings. After all, romance—in the full literary sense of the word—is not possible without an element of difficulty for the protagonists to overcome.

Again, I don't think I calculated all this logically, or even in full consciousness, at the time. Two days after our chance meeting, I flew to Los Angeles to work on the most troublesome of my several projects. I intended to call Libby from there to arrange a date and several times reached out to plug myself into the WATS line connecting the studio to New York, and each time found myself holding the receiver in an irresolute hand. Not knowing where she worked, I would have had to call her at home. All her children knew me and I was pretty sure that, having placed so many neighborly phone calls in recent years, they could probably recognize my voice. Obviously, I had a perfect right to call an old friend. Equally obviously, there was no particular reason to do so— except, as I guiltily imagined them imagining, that Mr. Koerner had evil designs on Mommy. A letter perhaps? I took out pen and paper. I felt foolish. Forget the whole thing? I resolved to do so. But wait a minute. Libby and I had scarcely fallen upon one another there in Bloomingdale's, tearing at our clothes and breathing hotly in each other's ears. Cool, correct, at most curious—that's how it had been. Fantasy had since outrun fact. But a long-distance call? In my business they were routine. In the lives of civilians they were not. They had a weight. Very well, then. I would restrain myself, call when I returned to New York. On the other hand, maybe a call from the Coast would impress her, convey an implication of interest that was more than casual. And scare her?

So I dithered. Like some footling adolescent. A forty-two-year-old man of some standing in his profession, some experience of the world. Drat.

It was my partner, Mort Kline, who resolved my confusion for me. Mort was a libidinous romantic, his pell-mell destiny shaped by a crazy energy that never permitted him to rest. Professionally and, as I was discovering, sexually, he was unable to prevent himself from pursuing any opportunity, however remote his chances of success.

We had spent most of the day screaming at each other—his habitual method of conducting business—trying to shape the structure for the middle section of the documentary film we were working on. Late in the afternoon we had sulkily split, retiring to our offices to reduce our conflicting opinions to memos. By the time I'd finished mine, my anger had cooled and I was willing to concede him a couple of points—as I knew from experience he was probably in the process of doing for me. Around five-thirty I wandered toward his lair—fake French provincial overlaid by the most incredible clutter of books and papers, some of them dating back three or more shows. He was not there and his secretary informed me he had gone for the day. I left my memo with her (if you left anything on Mort's desk, he simply mixed it in with all the other junk, thereby losing it forever) and told her I was taking off, too.

Emerging from the executive building and heading for my car, which was slotted in a visitor's parking space on the edge of the backlot, I saw Mort coming toward me. He was carrying a bunch of flowers—an unlikely sight. As he drew closer, I saw that they were quite an innocent arrangement—daisies and forget-me-nots.

"Heavy date?" I inquired.

"Naw," he said. "I'm not even boffing her." Mort had a way of getting right down to the bottom line, as we say in the business.

"So?"

"Just a nice lady I met."

"Flowers are a good idea," I said, thinking that I always forgot how much most women liked to receive them. If headlong, often thoughtless Mort Kline remembered them, I certainly ought to be able to.

"Flowers are essential," Mort said.

"So who's the nice lady?" I inquired, sensing that Mort was of a mood to talk, his favorite subject—women and the pursuit thereof—having been raised.

"Somebody I met at a party," he said. "Forty. Just divorced. Hurting."

Mort had broken up his marriage for a woman named Constance, who was as gentle as he was abrasive, as secure socially, professionally and economically as he currently was not, and very handsome. But she lived deep in the wilds of Malibu Canyon, where she profitably polished other people's screenplays, and they linked up mainly on weekends. This left him free to browse through the rich fields of the Greater Los Angeles area on week nights.

He looked at me shrewdly, this small, sharp-featured man, balding, pushing fifty, and anything but prepossessing. He said: "You should try it. If you're getting it regular somewhere else, of course. Just kinda have someone you take to dinner, maybe listen to some music with, be nice to without feeling you have to be dirty mauling her all the time. It's a relief for everybody."

"Then this is a purely altruistic activity on your part?"

He cocked an ironic eye at me. "Well, of course, it sometimes works out that way. But in hard times it can be like having a savings account to fall back on."

I laughed. Good old Mort. In the end, he always arrived at self-interest. Most of us do, of course, but what I liked about him was the speed and the lack of piety with which he got there.

We chatted on a few minutes, an aging roué and an unlikely one, exchanging tips on technique, leavened by the occasional colorful boast. All the while I was thinking that, whatever fantasies I had been entertaining, it would really be very nice to have a friendship with Libby of the kind Mort had been describing. I did not wish to exclude the sexual possibility— no fun in that, and it's unnatural anyway—but I did not wish it, either, to be at the forefront of our minds. Very confusing in our case. And anyway, what can be more romantic than self-denial—your basic Dante and Beatrice trip?

I rationalized. It seems faintly comic to me now, and appallingly lacking in self-awareness. But it was sufficient unto that day's problem. I marched back to the office and finally, finally, with only the normal amount of anxiety, placed my call to New York.

I beat the three-to-one odds that favored one of her children's answering the phone.

"Hello."

"Libby. It's David. Koerner"

"David? Oh, hi. Are you in town?"

"No. I'm in L.A."

"I thought so. You don't sound local."

"I've got this WATS line, so I thought I'd call all my buddies back there in the rain forest."

"It *is* wet. Nice out there?"

"Terrific. I've played tennis three mornings."

There was a pause—not quite an awkwardness, but potentially so. She filled the silence.

"How did the scarf go over?"

"I took the one you liked. It seems you have very good taste. But then, I always knew that."

"I never thought you noticed."

"Lots of people have thought that. They're wrong." I spoke more firmly than I intended. The words came out almost angrily.

"Little sore spot there?" She laughed.

"I'm a mass of bruises."

She did not respond. The awkwardness came upon us again.

"Listen, I'm coming back next week. I'm trying to arrange my social schedule, and I rashly promised you a dinner."

"My secretary's out just now, but I think I can fit you in."

"Name a night. You're at the top of the list."

"Wednesday O.K.?"

"You got it. Where shall I call you?"

She gave me her office number. Then she added: "David, the walls have ears down there. Have a time and place all picked out. I like to give yes and no answers."

"Right."

Another hesitation. "And, David . . ."

"Yes."

"No one needs to know—right?"

"Old friends have a perfect right to have dinner, don't they?"

"Natch. But how shall I say . . . there's a certain volatility in my situation. Anyway, I hate phones."

"Dig," I said. "Looking forward."

"Ciao," she said.

"See ya," I said.

When I hung up, my hands felt clammy, and anxiety had hollowed a small pit in my gut. If I had really believed that rationale I worked out for myself with Mort's help, I shouldn't have felt either. Physiology had betrayed me. I had, I'm glad to report, the good grace to laugh at myself.

Four

I was living, that spring, in a sublet apartment. I had taken it in haste and, since I had little leisure (and was often out of town anyway), repented it only on rare occasions.

The afternoon before Libby and I were to have dinner was one of them. It had been a month since I had done more than empty the ashtrays and throw out the old newspapers, and since I imagined we might return to my pad for after-dinner drinks, I thought it worthwhile to do some heavy tidying.

I am by nature neat, almost compulsive. But there was nothing about this apartment to encourage that instinct. It was located on the twenty-eighth floor of one of the slabs composing a "middle-income" housing complex in the Nineties on the East Side. The emphasis, on management's part, was entirely on assuaging modern urban paranoia. Grace never entered their calculations. Thus, we did not have doormen, we had pistol-packing guards, electronically leashed to one another by walkie-talkies, and of an evening, leashed as well to fierce dogs, with whom they menacingly stalked the cavernous, out-of-scale lobbies and the sterile corridors of the residential floors. These functionaries would not accept a package for you, not so much as a suit from the cleaner, if you were out. If, however, you were three days late with your rent check, one of them would accompany an assistant manager to your door to protect him while he posted, not a polite reminder to pay up, but a dispossess notice, signed by a sheriff's deputy. Fear and loathing thereupon led to terrible scenes in the management office, with tenants, who never in their bourgeois lives had been so served, threatening to punch their warders right out of their Robert Hall suits. Delightful.

The architecture of our overpriced apartments carried out the same warm, wonderful themes of the management style. In my place, for example, the kitchen "area" gave abruptly on the dining "area," which, in turn, flowed into the living "area." There were, for a wonder, doors on the bed- and bathrooms (I almost wrote "areas" again), but of course, the walls demarcating these spaces were the merest plasterboard conventions. Two or more people living in one of these hutches could not possibly have obtained any privacy. The man whose lease I had taken over for four months had not had time before his transfer to Phoenix to do more than minimal, functional furnishing. Throughout, post-collegiate Ethan Allen Colonial was fighting a foredoomed delaying action against the incursions of Swinging Singles Moderne. Neither style was my style, though, frankly, it had been so long since I had had charge of furnishing a home—or for that matter, even choosing all my own clothes—that I would have been hard pressed to say what, precisely, my style was.

Mostly, I did my best not to think about my surroundings. When I did, as I did that afternoon, Ajaxing the sinks and Windexing the windows and, finally, Mop & Glo'ing my floors, I found them distressingly suited to my general state of mind. I was not what I had been those many years and I was not what I thought—hoped—I soon would be. I was, like the two rooms in which I worked, neutral, slightly cold, underfurnished with leftovers and hand-me-downs from my former life and a few hastily assembled pieces suggesting not what was sure to come in the future, but a few vague ideas one had tried to formulate about it. There were those—including my former wife, who had dropped by one day to pick up her check—who suggested there was nothing wrong with the apartment that some pictures on the walls and some rugs on the floors would not put right, but they were wrong. The joint was conceptually flawed. And like a bad book or film—or life—there was nothing to do but abandon it and start over again before you wasted too much time on it. I blessed the brevity of my sublease. I could write all this off as a little experiment that hadn't worked out, walk through the door a couple of months hence, suitcases in hand, with not the slightest regret . . . only a feeling of relief.

It had not been my habit to live that way. But my anger at her beginning to die, I was also beginning to admire the strength of character it had required for my wife to treat our marriage not as jointly owned real property, an estate to be guarded for the security it would provide in the Sunset Years, but as a short-term rental to be gratefully abandoned for experiment with, as they say, "alternative life styles." I would never have been able to do it, left to my own devices. I would have stayed on forever in that decaying edifice, in that declining neighborhood, putting flowerboxes in the windows, rearranging the furniture, joining brave little committees that encouraged renovation . . . being strong and long-suffering, and *accepting* (a big word with me once) the pain and covering it over with a lot of existential bullshit.

The evidence of my conversion to a new, more transitory way of life seemed especially obvious to me that afternoon. It wasn't just that I began to whistle while I worked at my domestic chores, suddenly cheerful with my ridiculous living quarters. There was, as well, my changed anticipation of the evening ahead.

All thought of a sexual encounter now seemed well and truly dead, and even the possibility of establishing some sort of interest-bearing account with Libby seemed remote, a foolish notion suited perhaps to the way people live in exotic Los Angeles, but, like having a classically defined affair, not right, not quite in good taste, for Libby and me.

It was really quite simple: she was forbidden. I had no way of knowing just what her current relationship with Hilton, her husband, was, but I assumed since they were the most married pair any of us knew, ideal examples of the blessed state, that their separation must be no more than a temporary aberration. A gentleman, therefore, would not intrude upon whatever was going on between them. No, no. My dear chap. And anyway, Hilton Adderley was a very old friend, someone for whom I bore not the slightest malice. To take up with his wife, even if there was no hope of their reconciling, would be a needless affront, a deliberate hurt to someone I had no reason to cause pain.

But even setting that aside, it seemed to me, upon mature reflection—or what passed for it in those days—that whatever ambivalent signals we had sent out to one another up there in designer scarves, it was simply preposterous of me to have entertained the kind of fantasies that had lately bemused me. For there had always been something held back, enigmatic, about Libby Adderley, some very deep reserve that only someone far gone in hubris would dare to imagine penetrating.

I had known her as a girl, literally. I had known her as a young wife and mother. I had known her in her maturity. And I could not say that I had ever really known her. Nor did I know anyone who could believably assert such a claim. How could I now suddenly think that after something like two decades I was at last going to melt the wall of self-sufficiency, of slightly forbidding omnicompetency, that had through all those years surrounded her, protected her from the likes of me. By which I mean any friend, close or casual, who presumed an intimacy she had never to my knowledge granted anyone who was not blood kin.

The Adderleys. Stop to think of it, as I did that day, we probably should not have been friends at all. They "had money." That is to say, in the manner of their class ("good," but not great, Eastern Seaboard Waspdom) they possessed it in amounts that were never specified, but were obviously comfortable. They had been to the right raffish schools (Putney, Bennington, Bard) and their children looked to follow in their path. They took the right trips. They modestly collected master drawings, but did not call attention to them. Hilton, when he was younger, took the occasional job, thus proving to his extensive family, which seemed always to be hovering in the wings, checking on the younger generation's performance, that he shared their devotion to the busywork ethic (and, by implication, to the democracy of toil). Also, of course, the salary helped guard against the only truly abhorrent sin—"dipping into capital."

The trouble was, Hilton's dedication to familial principle was at best fitful. "Jobs are to quit," he used to say, and he was infinitely more faithful to that article of belief than he was to any other. Professionally, Hilton belonged to a type that was fairly common in New York in the fifties and early sixties. He was one of a number of bright, usually well-connected young men who always seemed to have the dummy for a new magazine in their knapsacks. Television had no appeal for them; that was for Jews and provincials. But print—print had a tradition, and it was explicable to relatives and friends, who could thus be more easily talked into financing a test-run of their dream, perhaps even a small office out of which to operate.

But in that time there was a sense that some of the old ways of doing business in the magazine world were coming to an end. *Collier's* had folded, the *Post* was fading, the big success stories were smaller, more specialized publications, which were fun to dream up, ought to be even more fun to manage. One could occupy oneself by doing something fresh and new, but not too fresh, not too radical. The trouble, for people like Hilton, was that the money to which they had easy access was not big money—and it tended to be very conservatively managed. They could always get seed money, almost as a handout, but they could never get the kind of dough they needed to bring in the harvest.

So a pattern emerged. He would busy himself with his latest idea for a year or so, then be forced to abandon it, then take a job for a while, until he was seized by some new possibility, whereupon he would cut loose again. Occasionally he would get fed up with the whole round and just take off six months or a year in some congenial precinct—Paris, Rome, San Francisco—where he would "do a little writing of my own" that never quite seemed to pan out.

No panic ever seemed to attend these peregrinations, and there was never any visible decline in the graciousness of the Adderley style, the ease of their manner. The wine was always good and plentiful, the children were always enrolled in the best schools, the hi-fi was always of the best, as was the art on the alien walls.

How did I—a workaholic of anonymous parentage, shaped by the paranoid populism of my native Middle West—fit with swells like the Adderleys? I suppose because when we were kids starting out in New York in the fifties, they seemed terribly exotic to me, as perhaps I did to them. We met when Hilton and I were working as very junior writers on a now defunct picture magazine. What had drawn us together was contempt for the place—its mean treatment of employees, its insensate treatment of the material it peddled the public twice monthly. Others in our station were either angry or earnest in their efforts to work for improvement "from within" (a fashionable strategy for dealing with institutions in those days). We affected, instead, an elegant contempt both for the magazine and for all other attitudes toward it (especially the earnest one). We also shared a conviction that somehow and soon something would happen to lift us out of that dismal place.

Libby was the lady I was eventually taken home to meet—brisk and efficient in the third-floor walk-up they were affecting in their young bohemian days. There, in the East Eighties, not as far from First Avenue as they would have liked, she admirably tended the child (now in college) whose crib shared their bedroom, produced excellent meals upon short (and often drunken) notification from after-work bars, quietly and patiently permitting our creative egos, swollen and aching in frustration, to spill their contents all over her living room in the long hours after dinner, when more drinking loosened the flow of quotations from the modern poets and the ancient movies. Her comments had always been brief and tart. Usually she had retired early.

We both quit the magazine around the same time. I took another job in New York, Hilton got one with a newsmagazine's bureau in Washington, and soon enough quit it for the longest of their several spells of expatriate life. Yet we kept in touch. I even gave him some assignments—indifferently completed—during a time when I worked as an editor. They were back in Georgetown when Marion and I married, and Hilton ushered at our wedding. Later, coincidentally, we rented a summer house on Martha's Vineyard and found them living in a house they had just bought in the next town. Day sails, picnics, expeditions in pursuit of wild strawberries and beach plums, ensued. Hilton was a venturesome, anecdotal companion, insisting only on some touch of elegance—pâté in the picnic hamper, or a very dry white wine, locally unobtainable but shipped in at the start of summer by a merchant he favored in Boston—to make the occasion memorable. He was always, in matters of style, one up on me. Or so it seemed. But never so much so as to make you resentful.

About Libby there was, as I say, this reserve. By the time of those Vineyard summers—the late sixties—they had three children, and Hilton's mother as a perpetual guest, and Libby managed their ménage as if she were the first officer of a minesweeper serving under a too-amiable captain, beloved by the ship's company but lax in discipline. She ran things tautly —more so than my wife did with only two kids under her command and no extraneous relatives. Meals were always ready at the appointed moment, the house never in disarray. Always friendly, she seemed never to come to rest, seemed always to be alertly scanning the area for some disorder to quell before it turned into disaster. Her intelligence, distinguished by a bullshit meter ticking quietly, constantly away, was as attractive as the slender elegance of her figure. And yet . . . she forbade. We soon learned that unscheduled pleasures were no pleasure to her. You did not drop in unannounced on the Adderleys. She never *said* anything. Her unhappiness would simply manifest itself in prodigies of housekeeping briskly pursued and giving visible lie to her protestations of welcome. In short, the Adderleys were a tricky lot, edgy. You had to be up for them.

In the end, though, they always seemed worth it. For they had style. They seemed, indeed, like characters left over not from the fiction of Fitzgerald or Hemingway but from their biographies. They were the kind of people with whom legends might have comfortably taken their weekends, the kind of people whose verandas seemed always to be blessed with a perfect afternoon light capable of bathing every snapshot in an enviable glow; there was always a feeling that the wine had been as perfectly chosen as the phrases of the conversation that flowed with it.

Around 1970, the Adderleys tired of Washington's insularity and returned to New York, where their youngest child and our eldest turned out to be classmates and—quickly—best friends in private school. Now, suddenly, children were being picked up and dropped off, the adolescent Adderleys were baby-sitting the little Koerners, and a friendship that had drifted into disuse was quickened. They had a lavish co-op on Park Avenue, bought with the last of Libby's capital, while we lived in an apartment in the Eighties that resolutely refused to grow as the children grew, demanding more space. One day Hilton called to say that a friend of his was anxious to make a quick sale on a brownstone around the corner and that it was a good buy. After a six-month period, during which I hocked all hope of discretionary income for seven years, if not a lifetime, we moved in. As it happened, on Halloween. Two months thereafter, Marion fell into a gloom self-diagnosed as a depression so deep its cure required that both of us to undergo therapy with that shrink I mentioned.

Poor fellow! He fought at our side in a gallant battle on several fronts: my suspicion of the entire process; the *Zeitgeist,* which supported Marion's strident assertion of her right not merely to liberation but to perfect and untrammeled self-realization (including, in her case, French and guitar lessons, extensive travel by herself, many gynecological consultations, and a course in self-defense, which provided her with the skills to chop away at those phantoms she imagined might deny her freedom); finally, there was the real-property syndrome to contend with. As yet this syndrome is unrecorded in psychoanalytic literature, but is familiar enough in the folklore of the modern middle class where it has been observed that the acquisition of a home—even a weekend cottage—inevitably places a strain on marriage. The organizing principle of the early years is, of course, striving, and the shared struggle forces a couple to ignore certain difficulties, encourages them to paper over problems with the belief that once they have achieved, arrived, those problems will naturally disappear. But a mortgage *is* arrival, and when the problems persist thereafter, you are bound to wonder what all the fuss was about all those years. For there you are, panting and sweating atop your plateau, and you don't feel a bit better than you did when you were struggling up the trail. Worse, all you can perceive from this vantage point is the trail back down, the one that winds only toward Sun City, the shuffleboard courts and the blackness beyond.

Unknown to me, something analogous was going on at the Adderleys', where Hilton had actually got a small literary magazine launched and was busily, happily, editing it, thus completing his passage to the brink of the mid-life crisis (God, the clichés that measure our years). But I knew little about his changing mood. Sugar, books, tools, advice, children, continued to be equably borrowed back and forth between the two homes. And Hilton was particularly helpful and comforting in the month after Marion—quite unilaterally— reached the decision that we must part, but before I could find a place to live. In that limbo of outrage and self-pity, Hilton poured the soothing drink, was ever available for the philosophical stroll. He hinted occasionally at strains in his marriage, but I imagined this was but a way of showing solidarity with me and that perhaps the reality of our separation had caused the fantasies of separation, always lurking not too far from the surface of any marriage, to rise to the top—imaginative chap that he was. I was quite genuinely surprised to learn, a couple of months later, that he, too, had moved out; thought to try to reach him; was too preoccupied by my own pain to do so; assumed anyway that so exemplary a marriage—a marriage on which so many acquaintances had based their certainty of that institution's stability—could not be permanently sundered.

Which brought my housewifely musings to date. Almost to *the* date, as it were. It's no wonder that women are so quirky and troublesome. Housework just does not fully occupy the mind, does it? I mean, it seems to encourage free flotation, a drift toward thickets of enigma, where one gets tangled in the unanswerables, the insolubles, leading either to terrible thrashings about or to desperate passivity.

It was in the latter mood that I put away my rags and brushes and bottles and took my shower and selected a clean shirt. I had thought too much about this meeting, had been up and down about it so much over the past couple of weeks that now, all things having finally been considered, the time having finally come, my mood was distant, objective. Lust, anxiety, even a sense of dramatic anticipation, had all been purged as I shut the door on my now sparkling pad. I felt myself observing myself as I walked down the street, imagined myself monitoring myself in conversation with Libby, making sure that I presented a proper image to her—mature and responsible, something we could both live with later.

It was, I admit, kind of a comedown from the mood I had

often anticipated for this night, but reserve, dignity, the qualities I had always observed in Libby, these were not to be sneezed at. I would, at the very least, not appear an idiot in her eyes, and that was something. Maybe it was all I could hope for in these difficult days—this coolness. As I turned into the street where the restaurant was located, I even felt a certain pride stirring in me, all fantasies having been consumed by their own heat, the ashes having been swept away by the broom I had so mightily wielded in the long twilight of the afternoon.

Five

The restaurant was not suitable, not suitable at all. That is to say, its mood, while perfectly suited to my earlier fancies, was not right for my present view of our encounter. It was very dim, with many small, well-separated tables covered in dark reddish cloths, the design of which surely suggested Provençal and may well have been authentically of that region. There were candles. I had used the place before for purposes of seduction, but now, with that thought firmly set aside, I was embarrassed to see how blatantly the place suggested its sexual usefulness.

I was on time, remembering Libby's famous punctuality, but she was more so, seated at a table in the farthest corner. I brushed her hair with my lips, caught a breath of very fresh, outdoorsy perfume. It was seven o'clock and only a few of the other tables were occupied.

"I had my choice, so I asked for the corner," she said.

"It's a guilty table."

"Guilty?"

"Sure. If anyone should see us, they'd immediately leap to the wrong conclusion. Innocence is best demonstrated by highly public acts. You should have taken a table in the center of the room, under a chandelier. If they had a chandelier."

She laughed. "Hilton always said you had a devious mind. He said that's why you're so successful."

"He's probably right. How is Hilton?"

"Hilton . . . is Hilton. Only more so."

"And how is Libby?"

"Coping. That's the short answer."

We ordered drinks, lit cigarettes.

"You look well," she said.

"Tennis tan. It fades fast. I think there's some peculiar reaction to New York smog."

"As opposed to L.A. smog?"

"Oh, that. Positively beneficial. Like low-tar cigarettes, which, as you know, actually prevent cancer."

The drinks arrived. We sipped appreciatively.

"Obviously things are good with you," Libby said.

"That's the convention I've started to maintain. I was in danger of becoming a divorce bore."

She smiled. I noticed she had extraordinarily white teeth. What an odd thing to notice.

"It's funny, isn't it? The minute you split, they start coming out of the woodwork. I haven't had so much free advice or heard so many horror stories since I was pregnant the first time."

"Yeah. One guy I hadn't heard from in years heard about me, called up, insisted on taking me to lunch. To tell me about *his* divorce. Seemed to think it was exemplary."

"And . . . ?"

"It wasn't."

The waiter appeared, ahover, and we ordered: soft-shell crabs and a salad. I asked for a carafe of house wine, for which I apologized after he departed. "I don't know anything about wine. I can't even remember the good years. To tell you the truth, I can't remember whether it's Bordeaux or Burgundy I think I like better. I know Hilton was good at all that."

"Wine bores are worse than divorce bores," Libby said. "It's a relief to order some plonk and be done with it."

She paused, cocked her head thoughtfully, then said: "Look, I'm out with you, not Hilton. Now, I know that in our particular case it may be hard to totally avoid him as a subject, but mostly I don't compare the guys I date with him."

She reached out and touched my hand briefly. "I'm here because I'm interested in you. In what's up with you." The last sentence she added quickly, so as not to leave an ambiguous sexual implication hanging in air between us.

I patted her hand in return. "And right back at you," I said.

"So, now," she said. "You are all hither and tither and I need to keep things straight. Where is it you go and what do you do?"

She smiled encouragingly, a very open and inviting smile. You could see in it the girl she had once been, I thought, a girl eager for news of the great world. It was almost as if she had suddenly told me a singularly revealing anecdote from her adolescence, and it somehow touched me.

So I told her funny Hollywood stories. And described for her conditions in economically battered London, which was, to my eyes anyway, as neat and orderly and splendid as ever. "The Stilton at Paxton's is unaffected by the falling pound," I said. "The Arabs don't actually hang their laundry out the windows at the Dorchester, whatever you may have heard."

Thus we occupied ourselves over the main course, the best part of which was the pungent salad. Over dessert, we turned to her.

She surprised me by telling me that their money had run out at just about the time their marriage had run down. Or virtually. "In time, of course, another of Hilton's relatives will kick the bucket. Meantime . . ."

Meantime, her job was not merely an exercise in mental health, something to stave off morbid thoughts. It was, she said, an economic necessity. What little they had left of their capital was pledged to retire certain debts Hilton had previously neglected to discharge. They needed her salary—she and the children—for groceries.

She spoke of these matters quietly, unemotionally. But there was in her tone a pride that would not be kept out.

"You know," she said, "I like it. I climb on the subway at eight forty-three and there's a sandwich in my purse and a *Times* under my arm. And I drift around Dry Dock Country on my lunch hour just like everybody else. I'm part of the human race. Finally. After all those years when Hilton insisted we were too fine for that sort of thing."

"But he has the magazine."

"It doesn't pay. Of course, he knows where there's some fresh capital. Meantime, he thinks he can take a couple thousand out of it by Christmas. Something of a shortfall, considering our needs."

I laughed, and so did she. And we passed on to other matters. Her kids. My kids. Gossip about some mutual friends.

How easy we were with each other. How unlike anything I had imagined this meeting was. Its subject matter inevitably reminded us of how old our friendship was, but the mood . . . the mood: I'm not sure I can describe it, it being a thing composed of gestures, tones of voice, something in her eyes and presumably mine. But somewhere along the way, the length of our friendship ceased to matter and we became, ironically, strangers to one another. But strangers who had taken an instant liking to each other, who wished to demonstrate their mutual interest without causing one or the other to shy off. It was, for me, like meeting a woman at a party, discovering instant rapport, and knowing, in the first moments of conversation, that I would ask for her phone number—and be on the phone next day. Except that I already had Libby's phone number.

We spoke much, rapidly, as if fearful that silence would spoil our mood, allow us time to remember why we should be awkward with each other. When the waiter brought coffee, he asked if we wanted anything with it. I looked at her inquiringly.

"Do you have Sambuca?" she asked. "It's a wild shot in a

French restaurant," she said to me, as he departed to check with the bartender.

"What is it?" I said.

"A whim," she said. "A whim with nice associations."

The man returned bearing two small glasses of clear liquid. He was visibly pleased with himself as he placed them before us.

"Better and better," she said.

"What are those?" I asked, eying the three brown, round objects in the bottom of each glass.

"Coffee beans," she said, "and correctly done, too. In Italy it's considered bad luck if they put an even number of them in."

She raised her glass and paused. I touched mine to hers and she kept her eyes on me as I tasted.

Licorice! "How did you know I liked Good and Plentys?"

"You looked the type," she said, something shy in her voice suddenly.

Now a silence did fall. She seemed lost in some memory and I did not wish to intrude. There was no need. A trust had grown between us. I knew that the evening would not finish when our drinks were finished. I did not know what would happen next. But I felt that whatever it was, it would be the right thing, and that we would not regret it.

Six

"Nice piece."

Request for permission granted, Libby had not paused for
further amenities, had stepped out smartly to inspect my apartment. There being nothing about it that was not entirely self-
evident, I had not accompanied her, contenting myself with
filling the drink order—brandy—I had elicited with a shout to
the bedroom.

Now, having snorted at the barren furnishings therein (I
don't think she opened the night-table drawer where reposed
the several copies of *Hustler* my landlord kept there, comfort-
ers to pull up around his imagination after a cold night in the
singles bars), having praised the excellent view of the Tribo-
rough Bridge and of the planes landing and taking off at La
Guardia beyond, she stood, hands on hips, in the center of the
living room, looking over the most remarkable of my furnishings—The Enormous Couch.

In all my born days I have never seen so massive an example
of privately owned modernism. Severe in line, high-backed,
high-sided and covered in reddish-brown corduroy, it filled an
entire wall in the living room. It was to other sofas what one
of those giant abstractions—a Kline or a Pollock—that can
only be hung in a spacious museum is to the painting of the

age—an expression of the *Zeitgeist* run amuck. It dominated, overwhelmed, ordinary surroundings—stuck out like a sore thumb. The accompanying ottoman, similarly swollen in scale, must have run the cost of the entire ensemble to something over two grand.

Libby advanced on the thing suspiciously, tested its cushions with a wary hand, then perched tentatively on its edge, as if afraid it contained some dangerous hidden mechanism. "Good morning. Procrustean Beds. Can I help you?" I said, and we both laughed.

"Old Howard, my landlord, is very proud of it."

"Well he might be. It's more than a couch; it's an investment."

Libby sank back on the sofa. Or tried to. The seat was too wide for her, tall as she was, to rest her back against the sofa's back and, simultaneously, keep her feet on the floor. She sighed, smiled and simply curled up in the corner of it.

She said: "You know, it's really rather touching."

"How so?"

"It sort of symbolizes faith in the future, doesn't it? I mean, someday he's going to have to get this huge, expensive place to go around his furniture."

"I guess so. Anyway, in the instructions he left taped to the refrigerator door, he specifically forbade making love on it."

"You're kidding. You mean . . ."

"He said it'd be all right if I put some sheets down. I'm not even sure a man and woman are allowed to sit on it unchaperoned."

"Why don't you risk it?"

"Will," I said, handing over her brandy finally. "For God's sake don't spill," I added.

"Howard should be happy. You're a good housekeeper."

"I'm glad you think so. I spent the whole afternoon at it, in case we came back here."

"Thought I'd run a white-glove inspection, did you?"

"Not really. But it did seem a value with you. In the old

days when we dropped in you always seemed to be cleaning or baking or something."

"With three kids and an alcoholic husband you have to keep up with things."

She spoke flatly, unemotionally. But that heavy word—alcoholic—crushed conversation for a moment. Finally, I said: "Alcoholic? In the full, lost-weekend sense of the word? Or just a heavy drinker?"

"We lost a lot of weekends. And some other things, too."

"Yes," I said. I looked inquiringly at her, but saw no sign that she wished to continue the subject. That was in character, and it pleased me. There is a dreary sameness about drunk stories, and you cannot pass as much time as I have in journalism and show biz without having heard them all. What interested me was that I had never thought of Hilton as a full-scale alcoholic. I am, of course, a prodigy of self-absorption and so tend to miss things that are obvious to everyone else, but for all the conversations that had tailed off into incoherence, for all the erratic comings and goings, it had simply never occurred to me to attach the harsh explanation to Hilton's quirkiness. Good breeding and a grand manner do tend to squelch subversive speculation.

"You know what I've decided lately?" I said. "I've decided that people are finally unknowable."

"Really?" said Libby, irony in her tone.

"I know that sounds sententious. What I mean is, I used to assume they were. Knowable. I figured the problem was with with me. Then, in the last few months, I started paying attention, really trying to dope them out."

"And . . . ?"

"Nothing. It's as hopeless as ever. There's some secret place in all of us that's just impenetrable."

"So you come out the same place."

"I suppose. But not really. It's sort of an obligatory existential errand, isn't it? Something we owe each other, and ourselves. To keep trying. It was the not trying that done me in

33

with Marion. It's maybe the only truly unforgivable sin."

What a fine speech—the more so since I really meant it at the time. I am capable, when properly stimulated, of such moral self-excitement. There is, God help me, this streak of idealism in me, and there is nothing like the presence of an attractive and sympathetic woman to bring it out. The trouble is that I get busy and tend to forget my principles, the upshot being that I'm always doing things I know better than to do, and feeling lousy about it.

Libby reached out and touched my hand. "You really are a nice man, aren't you?"

I'd heard that one before—usually in similar circumstances. But why fight it? If I wasn't always or even usually a nice man, I wanted to be, meant to be.

Libby made to withdraw her hand, but I held on to it. This was not meant as a preliminary to anything. I would hold her hand and go no further and prove the truth of her observation. This was more for my own benefit than hers—expiation of all the sweaty calculations I had made before our meeting.

She smiled almost shyly. "Hi there, good buddy."

"Hello," I said.

We sipped our drinks in a comfortable silence, continuing to hold hands. Finally, I spoke:

"How are you? Really."

"Fair to middling. That's the short answer."

"What's the long one?"

"Talk about unknowable . . ."

She tipped her head back, closed her eyes and sighed. I waited. At length she said: "I lived with him twenty years, since we were kids, and when he announced he was leaving it came as a surprise, a total surprise."

She paused again and added, fiercely: "I mean, man, we grew up together. Or didn't grow up. And I goddam didn't know. I didn't know until he was practically packing his overnight case."

Her anger was directed at herself, at the failure of a perceptiveness in which, obviously, she took pride and which, one gathered, had rarely failed her.

"Look," I said lamely, "we never know about the important things until it's too late. Then afterwards, all the clues we should have picked up . . . they become so painfully obvious. Literally painful."

Naturally, we felt compelled to rehearse some of this material, proving not so much to each other but to ourselves that we weren't as stupid as we must once have looked.

I told her that now that I thought about it, I actually knew my marriage was over almost two years before we separated. We had been going to the shrink together for a few months and suddenly a great gloom had settled over me. At first I could not understand its sources. We were finally talking, weren't we? Getting out in the open all the resentments we had silently conspired to bury through the years, confronting in an adult fashion our mutual problems. The books, the magazine articles, the very talk of the town, all assured us that we should be feeling terrific.

Why, then, was I skulking from movie to movie in midtown, noshing hamburgers at lunch counters, staying away from home until Marion was safely abed? The answer, of course, was simple. Marriages are based at least as much on tact, discretion, as they are on openness. And we were suddenly being forced to say unforgivable things to each other, things we would never dare say to a friend unless we were deliberately trying to rupture the relationship. Worse, it turned out that I was not good at this game, that I was incapable of firing the first volley or, having been fired upon, of wheeling the big guns around and answering shot for shot the withering fire that was being laid on me. God help me, it turned out I was more of a gentleman than I thought I was.

And more of a dullard. I had not known how deep my wife's secret furies were, or how wide-ranging. She was on a roll that spring, and once it was released, there was a depth and a continuity about her anger that was simply astonishing. I ran for cover and, unable to vent my answering rage, fell silent and morose, for what, after all, is depression but anger turned inward on oneself? I was, in the famous presidential locution, a mule hunkered down in a hailstorm. And though, finally, the storm somewhat abated, and we went on for a while, the damage—the irreparable damage—had been done.

God, have you ever seen such a jumble of metaphors? I really should rewrite the last two paragraphs, smooth them out, cool them off. But I'm not going to, for it was in some such tangle of phrases, surely, that I expressed myself to Libby that night. I am never inarticulate when, finally, I manage to speak my emotions—only sloppy with eagerness as I let them out. What surprises me, so much more time having passed, is that I still haven't found a language to express myself gracefully, originally, on this subject. Sputter, splutter.

"What a world we live in," I concluded. "The truth shall make us free."

"Well, it certainly did that, didn't it?"

I laughed. "Right on. But the thing is, it was all so goddam fashionable. You know, the articles in *New York* magazine about the new therapy, the peer group marching off, rank on rank, to scream I-I-I, me-me-me, under the auspices of some laid-back character in beads and beard."

"At least we skipped all that."

"Just an old-fashioned girl, aren't you?"

And, in a sense, she was. If mine had been a *Zeitgeist* divorce, the terms of our argument and our resolution all borrowed from such contemporary sources as *Ms.* and Erica Jong and the pop shrinks whose works pass through certain circles like an epidemic of dysentery in a summer camp, hers had a kind of classical symmetry about it. The way she put it was that the balance of power had shifted in her marriage. Or, perhaps more accurately, Hilton had made a unilateral attempt to effect such a shift. And had encountered unexpected resistance.

It happened like this: When he had finally got his magazine

going and actually held the first issue in his hands, proof at long last of his worth, he had decided to top himself. And so stopped drinking . . . pretty much, more or less. But suddenly clearminded, his absorption in his work ended, his eye free to roam over a familiar landscape that was newly transformed, or anyway seemed so to him, since he was beginning to pick out details (and even larger vistas) that had previously been obscure to him, he became, in his pride, "insufferable."

His basic discovery was that the way they had been living was, in his ringing phrase, "a hollow mockery." Libby tended to agree, but that was insufficient for Hilton, particularly since her assessment of the causes for their condition—tending to focus on Hilton's personality—was so radically different from his. He, naturally, blamed everything on her—"the whole damn twenty years"—and became aggressively critical of her day-to-day management of their home, their children, their lives.

It hurt. She had spent too many years apologizing for him, covering up for him, cleaning up after the emotional messes he left in his arrogant wake. To be criticized at this late date, and so sweepingly, had been too much for her. She had lashed back at him. The fights had got bad. And then they had merged into a continuous wrangle extending each day from breakfast to bed.

She sighed in the telling. "It *was* a power struggle. I can see that now. I can also see now that there was probably some way to compromise. You know, for a lot of years there, I'd have been glad to turn over all the responsibilities I'd accumulated; most of them anyway. I never especially wanted them: they just landed on me. Thud."

She turned away from me. Her words had come more haltingly toward the end of her speech, her tone had lowered almost to a whisper. Now, briefly, she seemed lost in reverie and I thought, though I could not be sure, that there was the hint of moisture in her eyes.

We sat silently for a time, and then I said that I thought the majority of marriages—certainly the older ones—were the casualties of such struggles. These days, I said, it was mostly the women who seemed to be making the power grabs, which made her case unique, if that was any consolation.

"But, yes," I added, "there ought to be a way of adjusting things, not tearing up two lives plus the kids. It's stupid."

"You had a shrink for a referee," she said. "What about that?"

"Nice try," I said. "But they're more into saving souls than saving marriages. If they have any decency at all, they tell you that up front. 'You may end up divorced anyway, but you'll understand why.' "

"And do you?"

"Just exactly as much as you do. Mostly I content myself with saying she was crazy. It's easier that way. And healthier. That's why I quit seeing the doc a month or so after I moved out. I just kept picking at the scab instead of getting on with the rest of my life."

"That's pretty much the way I feel," Libby said.

"And you're a few thou richer for skipping the couch. How's Hilton?"

"He's a moony recluse. When he's not being pissed off. Which occurs whenever I reject his little hints about reconciliation. That's what I meant when I said my situation was still volatile."

"You really don't want him back?"

"At first I thought I did. But I thought he ought to sweat a little bit. Revenge."

"And now?"

"I started enjoying my freedom. And I found out I was good at it."

"Don't we all?"

"No," she said, very flatly, very finally. "I think some people are just lousy at it. Their true colors come out."

She looked me straight in the eye as she spoke. And what I saw in her gaze was disappointment. She thought, I believe,

38

that adversity, isolation, would temper her man. So far, obviously, it had not. And what I read in her expression was a sad recognition that love's labor was irretrievably lost. It touched me enormously. I found myself wishing that I had sometime seen some similar expression in my own wife's features.

Touched, I touched her. On the arm. Her left arm. Just above the elbow. She responded by touching me in exactly the same place. Once again, our eyes met. But this time she closed hers—expectantly, I thought. And so I kissed her. Her lips were soft and open and invited my tongue.

We stayed so for what seemed a long time. We did not grab or grope or maul. We did not commit our bodies to this embrace. We were like children experimenting for the first time with this strange and powerful mode of expression that we had previously only heard and read about. We were ready to pull apart, to pretend that nothing had happened, if our emotions proved too strong (or too weak) to sustain this act of ours. Or if the censorious thought arose.

But there was only peace, a sweet stillness, between us. Surprise died. And puzzlement. And pain. For the moment at least, the dissonances of our lives, their broken rhythms—reflected in the tones and rhythms of our long conversation (which, of course, had settled nothing and revealed very little, come to think of it)—were resolved in some lovely chord that was beyond hearing, but not beyond feeling.

We pulled apart. We looked questioningly at each other. I took her by the hand and rose. She resisted. "No," she said. But I smiled at her, and she smiled back at me. And then she, too, rose and, still holding my hand, followed me out of that bare, flat-lit room, into dimness, into darkness, into forgetfulness, into some part of our futures.

Seven

"How, how to deal with love so we're not all blushing?" That's Virginia Woolf asking. And if it was hard for her, think how much more difficult it is for us today. After all, the literary conventions of a half century ago (and less) offered the writer some shelter from our current obligation to tell all and—if possible—imagine more. How pleasant for Virginia that she could, at certain moments, draw the blinds, close the door and tiptoe away from her characters, leaving them in blessed privacy, while herself running no risk of critical censure for her tact.

We, of course, labor under quite contrary conventional demands. Writers, readers, critics—we hold in common the deluded belief that the physical act of love offers profound insights into the personalities of the lovers, their existential condition, the condition of the whole damned universe, for that matter. It is the belief of the uncynical pornographer (and such a strange cat we have indeed bred in our time), a certainty that if, somehow, the camera can be pushed close, closer, closest to thrusting cock and receptive cunt, life's deepest mysteries will be revealed. Nothing of the sort ever occurs, of course. What really is revealed except those slight anatomical differences that are among the least important and least interesting factors individuating this man from that man, this woman from that woman? And, occasionally, such unwelcome intelligence as the fact that the leading lady had, on the day of shooting, a pimple on her ass? For the rest, we sometimes see animated some sexual position we have only seen frozen in one of those illustrated sex manuals that are the pillow books of our age. Or get to witness two or more people acting out in public some fantasy, usually involving assistance from the animal or vegetable kingdom, that we have previously only imagined in private. Basically unedifying stuff.

Certain things about Libby's love-making you can, if I have been accurate and intelligently selective in my reportage, already imagine. You know, don't you, that such a woman would kindly but firmly brush aside my fumbling attempts to assist her with buttons and snaps, would instead take up a position in the center of the room and briskly and efficiently strip herself, neither hiding nor flaunting any part of her body as it was revealed to me, backlit by the city's slight night glow spilling in from the unshaded window behind her? And me? Of course you know that, as my eyes adjusted, became aware that the darkness was not as total here as I had imagined, I stopped, one sock off, one sock on, to watch her, not as a voyeur, sneakily, but in a kind of romantic awe, as open in its way, I suppose, as she was in her exposure of herself. There being nothing of the tease about her, there was a kind of classic grace to her movements as she brushed her clothes away, pausing only to drape them neatly over a canvas chair nearby.

When she was nude, she crossed to the bed, where I was sitting, and stood before me, hands at her sides. She allowed me briefly to explore, with hands and mouth, the curves of her hips and thighs and belly, stopping me gently when I tried to press on to a greater intimacy. "Not yet," she said. "Not until I can get at you."

And so, quickly, with a degree of furtiveness, since I had been taught in marriage not to think especially well of my body, I scuttled out of my remaining clothes and scrambled to join her under the covers. We kissed very deeply, our fingers straying over one another's bodies, and while my tongue searched deep into her mouth, I felt one of her fingers slide into my . . . ear! Oh, pornographers, dear hearts, what do you make of that? What do you make of my confession that no one had ever touched me so, that I had not even read or heard about it (we are not talking here about adolescents hopefully, earnestly *blowing* in each other's ears, understand)? Doubtless that I had led a singularly deprived sensual life. What do you make of the fact that of her many ways of touching me, this is the one I most miss, this caress that was at once so innocent and so knowing? Doubtless that my naïveté is hopeless, incurable. So be it.

I could amuse the prurient, I know, by rhapsodizing on the far more intimate discoveries of this evening. I have, indeed, in my first draft, a very fine poetic passage describing in wondering and loving terms certain details of Libby's person, certain intimate contours and textures that filled me not quite with ecstasy when I first encountered them, but certainly with a glow of happy satisfaction, that fill me now, as I think about them, with a longing that is almost painful. A tall woman, as I have said, she was yet the most delicately formed of women in that region where words (quite properly) fail us—the clinical terminology being hopelessly out of tune with one's feelings, the common slang being equally jarring in a different way, D. H. Lawrence to the contrary notwithstanding. I said that physically, she filled me with happiness, satisfaction, and I was speaking precisely. It was not that the reality of her body perfectly matched my fantasies (who can predict the appendectomy's scar, for example?), but rather that reality did not quarrel with fond expectation in any significant way, administered no nasty shocks to it. And so a kind of anxiety was stilled, a predictable stage in the drama reached without the playwright's startling us with an exercise in ingenuity. She was as I hoped she would be.

On this point I shall say no more. In a sense we are talking about a lucky accident. Libby Adderley was not privy to my fantasies, could have done nothing either to enhance or diminish my pleasure in her physical being. Nor could I possibly have reciprocated. All we could say was that we felt good about one another's presences from that first moment when we began to shed clothes and inhibitions, and that whatever happened between us later, we continued to feel that way.

We were patient with one another, and easy. Having committed ourselves to what seemed to us, cultural laggards that we were, a definitive act, we did not rush, did not demand of ourselves more than we could decently grant the other at any given stage of our love-making. I think we knew instinctively that, in the end, each of us intended to give all that it was possible for us to give, which is just a way of saying that there was, from the instant we lay down together, unshielded, able to see and touch without inhibition, great, if not total, trust.

All of that is, I think, incommunicable, and properly so. What passed between us now passed in virtual silence. We seemed to know precisely how to touch one another, how to pleasure each other without awkwardness or small, painful accident. What she communicated to me through her responses to the questions I posed with my hands and lips and body was a preference for direct and uncomplicated sexual communion. There was something very simple about her way of expressing herself sexually. It was not the naïve simplicity of youth; it was, rather, the refined simplicity of maturity. She was, I suppose, like one of those artists who have discarded the mannerisms born of their early technical virtuosity in favor of a kind of bold artlessness.

We were strangers, we did not yet know one another's rhythms, but as I have no need to assert my masculinity by imposing my pace on women, I was content to follow her lead. Content? No, the word is too feeble. I wished, very simply, to give her precisely what she wanted, to serve her needs so that I could learn what they were. I do not for a moment believe I am the stud of the sex manuals' dreams, but anatomy alone should teach us the obvious fact that a woman's sexual gratification is more difficult to attain than a man's. Good Lord, the latest studies seem to indicate that for the majority, a length of plastic surrounding a couple of batteries and a primitive jiggling device is preferable, from the standpoint of efficiency, to that huffing, puffing bundle of egocentricity known as the American Male. It is a very chastening bit of information, that, and it seems to me that the best thing we can do, until we know our lovers intimately, is to let them use us as they will. Indeed, it seems to me the quickest, surest way of learning how to please them. And you know what? It is very pleasurable—the lack of responsibility, I mean, the abandonment, in the very moment of conquest, of the arrogance of the *conquistador.*

But yet . . . there came a moment when Libby ceased to move beneath me, when I felt her relax, not in triumph but in puzzlement. I opened my eyes and looked into hers and she said: "I'm sorry."

"For what?"

"For taking so long. I don't usually. . . ."

"Not your usual situation."

"I can't stand being a bore."

"You're not," I said.

Gently, by unspoken mutual agreement, we disengaged. I stroked her hair and she rested her head on my chest. She thus hid her face, and I realized that she was embarrassed. Libby Adderley, competent in all things, her pride a function of that competence, feared that she appeared incompetent in this most significant of activities.

I pulled back slightly, lifted her chin, and said: "Speed has never seemed a virtue to me—not in love anyway."

"First times," she said. "First times are hard." She looked at me questioningly.

"Yes," I said.

She looked away then, and after a moment I touched her on the shoulder.

44

"Libby," I said. "Libby, do you understand? I love being in you. And I can wait as long as you need me to."

Again, that dubious, questioning expression. "It's my one parlor trick," I said. "Bedroom trick, I mean. I really love to show it off."

She laughed, and hugged me, affection—that mild and useful emotion, until then blotted out by other concerns—in her embrace.

Now when I touched her she rose to me, making minute adjustments in the position of her body to indicate precisely where she needed my fingers, then, in time, guiding them with her hand, setting the motion and rhythm she wanted. A little later, she pulled me into her. Briefly, she was all fierce concentration, entirely acceptant, at last, of her own selfishness.

But so quiet. There were never any wild cries of passion with her, no gasping for breath. You had to listen hard for her climaxes. "Oh," she would say. "Oh . . . oh . . . oh." Never anything more. But her quiet compelled my concentration, brought us, usually, together to the end. As happened this first time.

In fiction, in those case studies of the sexually troubled that now proliferate, in porn, this is made to seem a big deal, the most astonishing triumph of the will, as it were. It never seemed so to me, to us (I think the plural is justified, though I don't know, since we never felt any need to talk about all this). The implication, after that first awkwardness, was that it was our natural right, nothing we had to worry about or strain toward.

Have I talked too much? Have I violated my own contemptuous view of the tell-all spirit of the times? Have I, in the enthusiasm of delightful reverie, turned unwitting pornographer? I suppose I have. Character is not monolithic, is it? God knows, mine isn't.

Yet in a way I've proved my point, I think. There is nothing we learned about each other in bed that we could not have learned—had not already begun to learn—in conversation; for that matter, by going to basketball games together. Sex is just a metaphor, isn't it, a way of focusing, intensifying, otherwise inchoate feelings. That's why, artistically speaking, this chapter was inevitable, essential.

And, all posturing aside, irresistible for the author, one of those habitual scribblers, for whom nothing is real, or permanently fixed, until he has written it down, fixed it on paper, where he fondly imagines its shelf life will be longer than it might be in that Fibber McGee's closet that is his memory.

The important thing, the absolutely vital thing, he has to remember is that in that hour everything was blotted out: that silly apartment, the man from the IRS arguing with his tax lawyer, the stewardess insisting that his comfort and safety depended on keeping his seat belt fastened until the plane came to a complete stop at the gate, his children's unpaid orthodontia bills, his sometime wife exacting reparations for war damage; the whole panoply of self-important intruders on his life. He had achieved such blessed forgetfulness for a moment, for five minutes, with other women, but with none had it been so total, so capable of infinite extension. With none, he would discover, could he be as sure, before the fact, of achieving this gift of renewal. He would always wonder if it was the same with her. And hope so, fervently hope so.

Eight

We lay now in a shy silence, fingers lightly intertwined. I
cannot recall my thoughts in any detail and I don't know hers.
I was afraid to break that silence, for such words, fragmentary
phrases, as occurred to me were clearly inadequate to our
mood, certain to shatter it.

I think the simplest word to summarize my feelings is
"awe." It doesn't quite fill the bill, but it's as close as I can
come. The first and only time I indulged in an extramarital
affair, I felt the same way, knowing that something of unpre-
dictable, but large, consequence had occurred, that it was not
something I could ever in the future dismiss with some cool,
casual phrase or offer up as a kind of initiatory boast to the
great fraternity of middle-class Casanovas that is always implicitly asking you to join up.

Setting that aside, it seemed to me that a certain tact was
now required of me. It is always easy to dismiss the single
encounter. You know the kind of excuses we make: I had too
much to drink; he/she seemed so sort of sad and lonesome,
I just felt sorry for him/her; I don't know, something just kind
of came over me. And then: I felt depressed for a week; at
group they really disapproved; I mean, I actually felt *immoral,*
can you believe it? And finally: Never again. Given the quality

of the beginning, I thought we deserved a better ending than something along those banal lines. And of course, I wanted a long, lovely middle passage—it could stretch to infinity, as far as I was concerned at that moment—and I imagined she did, too. But I felt, as I was to feel often in the months to come, that I must give her no excuse to shy away. For throughout the evening I had been picking up little signs of skittishness: nervous gestures, sudden silences; nothing really alarming, I suppose, but something that seemed nevertheless to require some sort of unspoken reassurance in response.

Just what that should be I had no clue, and so continued to maintain radio silence while patrolling our emotions. It was she who broke that silence.

"I wouldn't have given you up," she said. Her face was turned away from me as she spoke, and her voice was sleepy, thoughtful.

She turned toward me, and her large brown eyes seemed even larger than usual. And far softer. There was a vulnerability in them that I had not seen before, and again I thought I could glimpse in them the child she once was, whom I had never known. She touched me on the chin, lightly ran her fingers along the line of my jaw, and it seemed to me that she was trying to assuage *my* anxiety, clues to which, I suddenly realized, I must have been giving off as surely as she had been.

I touched her hair, which she wore very short. I smiled at her. "You might have," I said.

"Might have what?"

"Might have given me up."

"Whatever for?"

"Because I don't think I was very generous to Marion. Not in the ways you mean."

"Mea culpas are so dismal."

"Not making one. Somehow, we never meshed quite right. Do you know what I mean?"

She made a questioning gesture. I said, "There was something mean in me. I was a sort of emotional string-saver.

48

Maybe I still am. Anyway, she brought out that side of me. I brought out a part of her that was, I don't know, maybe not quite moralistic, but disapproving."

"Still," she said, "you've always seemed to me a very generous man."

"Always?"

"I used to watch you with your kids. And with mine."

"Kids are easy, in a way. Their demands aren't very complicated."

"No, I suppose not." She turned away from me again. "But I'm pretty sure I wouldn't be here if I hadn't thought of you that way."

Unaccountably, I felt tears tingling in my eyes. And where is your blue-eyed cheerfulness now, Mr. Wonderful? the conventionalized optimism, blithely heedless of past hurts, that so distinguished your pillow talk with the others (dear Ellen excepted). The solvent of knowledge applied to it, it simply disappeared like one of those greasy stains in a pseudo-scientific commercial for some detergent.

"Discovered at last—my dirty little secret," I said.

"Do you have a cigarette handy-by," she said. "Mine are in my purse way out there."

I rose and groped through the pile of clothing I had left on the floor at the foot of the bed. The cigarettes were in my coat pocket; the lighter had fallen out of my pants pocket and, when I recovered it, refused to light until I had flicked its little metal wheel a dozen times. I lit the cigarettes simultaneously, Paul Henreid style, passed one to her and hopped back into bed.

My homely little errand broke the incipient self-pity of my mood. I asked: "Generosity? Is it important to you?"

"To everybody."

"Sure. But you know what I mean. It's not the first word that springs to mind. In the present context."

"No, I suppose it isn't." She paused thoughtfully. "I guess it *is* terribly important to me right now." She stopped again to choose her words. "Divorce is such an ungenerous business, isn't it? All those years of trying to share things equally. And then, suddenly, your lawyer is fighting for every ridiculous little advantage and so is his. And worrying about the remotest contingency. As if someone you've known all your adult life is suddenly a psychotic master criminal determined to reduce you to penury. Meanwhile, you know the other side feels the same way about you."

She was right, of course. It's the pettiness of it all that wears down your spirit. And leads right-minded people to make bad settlements just to end the niggling and nagging. Paradoxically, it also leads other right-minded, perfectly nice people to sustain the struggle until they have gained the last cent they can in the settlement, the last extra minute of visiting rights, precisely because they have seen people every bit as nice as they are done in by a former spouse who really has turned psycho, or has been led into a reasonable facsimile of that condition by a gun-slinging divorce counsel. What a work is man. And woman.

"The other side," she repeated. "Imagine thinking about a man you were married to for twenty years as 'the other side.' You see what I mean? About the importance of generosity."

"Yeah," I said, watching her tug the covers up under her chin.

I took her in my arms. "I'll try always to be generous with you," I said.

"Same here," she said, and we kissed.

When we pulled apart she said: "Could we sleep? Just for a few minutes? Then I really have to go."

"Not on my account."

"No," she said. "On mine."

Her voice was dimming, yet it was firm. I knew she would not be spending the night, respectable lady that she was, with children who would wonder why she was not at the breakfast table tomorrow morning—this morning, actually, I saw as I took her cigarette from her and stubbed it out with mine in the ashtray that stood next to the digital clock-radio on my night table.

She slept. I dozed, excitement pulling me back from sleep whenever it threatened to fully enfold me. I could not bear the thought of surrendering to it, losing even a moment of this night to it. My right arm was caught between her head and one of the pillows, my left hand was outside the covers, resting lightly on her hip. Her head was snugged against my shoulder, so that when I breathed I lightly stirred the hair on the top of her head. Her own breathing quickly deepened and slowed and she was otherwise terribly still—trusting, it seemed to me —as she lay in my arms. Whether she was or not—maybe she was just one of those people who catnap easily—I felt very protective toward her.

We had begun to hint at our hurts and I knew enough about mine to understand that hers matched them in the continuing strength of their afterlife—the sudden blips of anger that appeared out of nowhere, the equally sudden descents into sadness, that rawness of spirit that causes the most ordinary things to touch you with extraordinary intensity: a young mother ministering to a crying child, as one once did and now does not; a family group on a Sunday stroll, children chattering, parents comfortably bored as they answer their questions; a guidebook to Versailles, souvenir of a happy week in Paris, found in a carton of books your ex insists she cannot store a day longer in her rearranged house. I judged Libby and I were both past overt self-pity, but these small, secret nostalgias, these brief, private stirrings they created—these were still present, reminders that one had yet a way to go.

What I thought was that Libby and I could in a sense complete the process of recuperation together and that, knowing each other as well as we did, we could do so almost wordlessly. I was so tired of words, of rehearsing my boring, aging tale of woe, and so was she, I imagined. Maybe, sympathetic and intelligent people that we were, maybe we could help each other on to the next stage, the one where once again you habitually looked forward instead of back.

She stirred. "Nice," she said. "Gotta go."

But she did not move. "Libby," I said, "I've been thinking. Could I call you Elizabeth?"

"Sure," she said, "but what's the point?"

"It's all terribly symbolic. See, I've always thought of you as Libby. But now . . . Well, now you're different. To me anyway. And besides . . ."

"It's a girl's name, isn't it? Not very matronly." She laughed.

"I wasn't thinking of you quite that way."

"I know. But I sometimes do."

I kissed her. And not as a matron either. Nor did she respond as one.

"Now what, Elizabeth?" I said.

"Now? Now we put on our clothes and you walk me to a discreet corner a couple of blocks from my house and you tell me you'll call me next week and I tell you that'll be fine."

"That's it? I can't call you tomorrow? Or make a date for Saturday night?"

"No, no and no." And then she kissed me and sat up. She made as if to swing out of bed, then paused and turned to me.

"Listen to me a minute, will you?"

"Of course."

"I won't pretend I'm surprised to find myself in your bed. I thought we might end up here—if things went right between us, I mean. The only thing that worried me was . . . entanglement."

"Sure. I can see that."

"I'm not sure you can."

"O.K. Try me."

She settled back, plumping a pillow behind her. "Just lately," she said, "I remembered something. When I was a little girl somebody sent me a postcard from Switzerland. I kept it tucked in the edge of my mirror, over my dresser, for the longest time. There was this little toy village, all bright and

52

cheerful, little people hurrying through the main street, intent on their business. But it was nestled against this huge mountain, vast and mysterious. . . ."

"And . . . ?"

"I don't really know why I liked it so much. I guess it was the snug and the forbidding right next to each other. Or the known and the unknown. Something like that. Anyway, that picture popped into my mind a couple of months ago. And I *do* know what it means to me now."

"Yes?"

"I feel like I've been living in that village all my life, all snugged up in my safe little assumptions about what life was all about, what was expected of me."

"And then the mountain fell on you?"

"No, that's not it, smarty. I feel as if someone sprung all the locks and I'm setting out on the trail up the mountain. And I'm frightened and exhilarated and I know I have to keep going. At least until I can see the next valley."

"You should never climb alone. All the books say so. You should be roped to at least one other climber."

"Yes, I know. But this is just a metaphor, not reality. And I've had enough of ties—for a while anyway."

She took my face in her hands and smiled tentatively, inviting my understanding.

"Yes," I said, "I think I get it. I don't know why, but yes."

"That doesn't mean I wouldn't like to meet some people along the trail," she said. "Or even that we couldn't go part of the way together if things worked out."

"That's good," I said. And then I took her in my arms again, a gesture of encouragement, of solidarity, if you will. And then we began, quite unthinkingly, to touch one another and then we passed from affection to urgency and we made love again, quick and fierce, reasserting the truth of this hour against the ambiguities of the future, making a small certainty we could cleave to amidst the uncertainties of events, of ourselves, in time to come.

And then it was as she said it would be. I took her most of the way home and we agreed to let a little time pass before we spoke again. And if we made no promises about our next meeting, I knew, as we parted, that we had made no promises to avoid it either. It was, I thought, enough. Not all that it might be, but enough.

Nine

The phone shattered my sleep, which had been deep and dreamless, as completely restful as any I had known for a year and more. A glance at the clock informed me that it was 9:07 and that it was my late wife calling. No one else I knew was in dialing condition before ten. I shuffled to the living room and the ludicrous princess phone—not the instrument of choice among us heavy-duty telephonists—and scooped it up, jangling in my hand, from the floor, the while trying to mobilize my sense of irony. It, however, was still piling up Zs in its lair and refused to come out so early in the morning. I was hard pressed to manage a falsely wakeful hello.

"David? Marion. I hope I didn't wake you."

"Up for hours," I replied, the hoarse croak of the coffeeless betraying my lie.

"Do you have a minute?"

"Sure. Just let me get a cigarette."

I didn't want one, but I needed a moment to make a mental adjustment and I knew that at some point in the conversation she would manage to raise my anxiety, or my anger, to a point where I would need to suck on something, and a thumb is, I feel, *infra dig* at my age. I also grabbed a bathrobe to ward off the impending chill and, as I padded back to the phone, wondered why one was always being forced to make rude transitions in this life.

"What's up?" I said briskly.

"It's not so much what's up as what's down. Namely, my bank balance."

So it was to be *that* conversation. It was marginally more agreeable than the one where she importuned me to take the children for a long weekend so that she could go off with some lover, then accused me of a lack of proper fatherly emotion when I refused. That one created an exquisite tangle of ambiguous feelings that could only be resolved in a great primal scream. This one would also end in outrage, I imagined, but it would be of a simpler, more straightforward kind.

"Yes," I said. "I thought I was paid up to the end of the month."

"Well, there's the refrigerator. I told you about that."

"Something about the freezer compartment."

"Yes. And then there's this doctor's bill."

"Wait a sec. I just paid a bill from a Dr. Clements."

"That's the gynecologist. This is Feldstein. He's a GP."

"I don't suppose you could arrange some sort of one-stop shopping?"

"David! We're talking about my health, not the Bloomingdale's bill."

"Sorry. Didn't know you were sick."

"I'm not. Except I've been feeling kind of run-down. And there was that weight loss. I mentioned that to you."

Actually, she'd looked just fine the last few times I'd seen her, but that, of course, was a strictly nonprofessional opinion. What I knew for a fact was that there had been an extraordinary run of medical expenses—quite outside the pattern of our married years—since I'd moved out. Dentists, optometrists, even a podiatrist had been consulted in the last six months. And she was still checking in twice a month with our psychiatrist.

"Every cloud has a silver lining," I said.

"What is that supposed to mean?"

"Nothing. Just that I wouldn't mind losing ten or fifteen pounds in all this."

"God, you're impossible."

Doubtless I am. But it seems fair just to note for the benefit of the objective reader that we were stumbling around here in a gray area. Lacking a formal separation agreement, I had written her a letter outlining those expenses over and above the allowance I provided monthly, which I would bear until our lawyers had concluded their stately minuet. I had said that I would take care of emergency repairs on the house and unusual medical bills. Routine maintenance of house and self was her responsibility. As it happened, and as I should have imagined, everything turned out to be, in her view, an extraordinary occurrence—my responsibility, not hers.

I pointed out the curious contrast between her present state of constant medical crisis—a crisis that, judging from the bills, was also infecting our children, their bouncy manner to the contrary notwithstanding—and our formerly placid relationship with the medical fraternity. She countered with the observation that keeping her healthy was in my best interests. "Just like any employee," she added.

"Oh, let's not start up with that," I said wearily, for she was much taken with the fashionable notion that a woman was entitled to something like workman's compensation for taking care of home and children, just as if it were a regular nine-to-five job (with, to be sure, a lot of overtime). Myself, it seemed to me that a traditional marriage, which ours had been, with the wife enthusiastically volunteering for this duty initially, was essentially a team operation, with a division of labor taking place between its members. True enough, she had wasted many a good hour getting the kids to and from their friends' houses, their lessons, what have you. On the other hand, I had not forced her out into the cruel midtown streets, into the corridors of petty power, there to treat endlessly with assholes in order to obtain the work by which we sustained our rickety life style. It was a wash, as far as I was concerned. And it was especially so now when—liberated promises so quickly forgotten—she had done nothing to ease the financial load, which had, of course, grown enormously since we began leading separate lives. I decided to forgo pointed questions about her mythical search for a part-time editorial job, or free-lance work. I decided to stick to the specific point.

"Just how much, exactly, does this Feldstein require?"

"Well, it's one hundred and fifty, plus the lab bills, of course."

I bit back a cry of pain. "Marion, you've just got to find a less expensive hobby."

Yes, I know. I should have chomped down on the sarcasm, too. Counterproductive. Unworthy of me. Worst of all, stupid, for I was in a negotiating situation, my objective being not to score cheap points, but to get the best possible deal I could out of our exchange. It is manifestly impossible to negotiate with rage.

I let her run on, through my crassness, my insensitivity, my lack of common decency, my moral numbness, all those views of my nature that were so refreshingly at variance with my own self-evaluations. Somewhere in that faintly comic description of the ex-husband as S.S. *Oberführer*, however, I picked up the key phrase: "I mean, for godsake, I haven't had a thorough checkup in six years."

"Whoa," I cried. "Checkup? What you had was a checkup?"

Pause. "Well, yes, of course."

"I refer you, then, to paragraph four, subsection A, of my letter of Jan. eighteenth, inst."

"What are you talking about?"

"The letter. The infamous letter. In it I specifically exempted myself from paying for them."

"But I told you. I was run down."

"Who isn't?" I said. "You gotta say something to doctors

or they think you're crazy for sitting around their offices in a little paper robe."

More splutter. To which I listened with growing self-contempt. Here I was, arguing with a woman I had loved, and more than that, liked, for almost all of the fifteen years we had been married, someone who had comforted me in failure, struggled with me for success, had possessed wit and style and comeliness which I had found agreeable and well suited to my taste; here I was, behaving with the meanness of some Dickensian villain to a woman with whom—dare I admit it?—I would still, at that point, have attempted reconciliation if she had shown the smallest sign of interest in that course; here I was, squabbling over a lousy one hundred fifty bucks, a sum that any reasonably competent jurist would have awarded her without thought. It was madness.

Specifically, it was a form of paranoia. Money is virtually the only interesting subject left to divorced couples (assuming a modicum of good will where the children are concerned), and so, to your discussions of it, you bring all your left-over emotions, all your gloomiest suspicions, darkest fears, whiter-than-white angers. You no longer know what the other party is up to, but you do remember all his or her former unfairnesses, selfishnesses, thoughtlessnesses. Not knowing if they have changed or grown (and, indeed, hoping they have not, so that you can sustain, through the issuance of the final decree, your belief that you're doing the right, the only, thing), you immediately assume bad faith, yet another attempt to do you dirt. She assumed, for example, that I passed all my nights in (her phrase) "expensive midtown restaurants," attempting myriad seductions, the expense of which removed bread from our children's mouths. I, on the other hand, was certain she wished to have me take up permanent residence in a Booth cartoon, in that apartment where the naked light bulb dangling from a ceiling cord illuminated cracked plaster walls and a few sticks of Salvation Army furniture. Having, on advice of counsel, cut off most of her charge accounts, it seemed to me that her sudden access of concern over her own and the children's health represented an attempt to exploit and expand the one loophole I had left her habitual extravagance.

All these points we raised anew, and the vindictiveness of our tones, the sheer nastiness of the squall we were conspiring to raise, sent me from self-loathing to depression. If I could have, I would have banished these foredoomed attempts to achieve *ex post facto* emotional justice through fiscal policy, would have settled upon her what used to be known as "a handsome sum," buying with it the gift of silence between us. The only joint property we held that was of any value was memories, and it seemed to me each conversation of this sort stained them, obscuring their patterns, diminishing their meaning and worth. Anyway, she was entitled to her psychosomatic ills, wasn't she? In the first months of separation we all seek—and will spend any amount to find—reassurance that we are not mortally damaged. My dinner dates, her doctors —they came to the same thing: a search for some objective observer who, upon studying the evidence, would inform us we would, after all, live.

So I said: "How about halvesies?"

"What?"

"Why ruin both our days discussing it? I'll split Feldstein's bill with you, and throw in the freezer compartment."

"You are the soul of generosity," she snapped. Not exactly a graceful concession, but, I judged, a concession nevertheless.

We both fell silent. It is a form of extravagance unique to the twentieth century, sulking on the telephone, a conspicuous consumption of electronic technology never intended to deal with the subtleties of nonverbal communication.

"Well," she said finally, "I guess that's it."

"Until next time," I said wearily. "I'll send you a check."

We hung up without saying good-bye, the conventions of common courtesy often being simply more than either retired spouse can handle on certain occasions. I made my humble breakfast—orange juice, toast and coffee—retrieved the *Times* from outside my front door and, not surprisingly, found nothing of interest in it. I sipped a second cup of coffee and stared out the window. There was a swell view of another high-rise abuilding across the street, and there were some steelworkers toddling suspensefully about on its naked girders. Somehow I could not even awaken my usually lively acrophobia and get it interested, as it generally was, in their fates. That left the crossword puzzle, but it had distressingly long horizontals this morning and I abandoned it after a few minutes' desultory doodling.

Down. Flat. Inexplicably sad. Or maybe explicably. Just for a moment here, the past had become the future, and the future suddenly seemed past. To put the matter less enigmatically: I had been feeling for some time that I had finally managed to put Marion's claim on my emotions entirely behind me. For several weeks now we had managed a decent imitation of civility in our occasional contacts and I had begun to foresee a time when, memories of our last years together no longer lively, we would cease the attempt to exact reparations from each other. After this phone call, however, the dread vision of endless petty acrimony, extending onward, ever onward into geriatric infinity, recurred. I saw myself struggling up through the morphine administered in massive doses to ease my passage through terminal illness, to answer a phone call in which the voice of my sometime wife, now cracked with age, pointed out to me that the alimony check was three days late.

That's what I meant about the past becoming my future. As for the future becoming the past, I gloomily imagined that it had already happened, that Elizabeth on this morning after had decided that the night before represented your classic moment's madness, that the practical difficulties of building on what we had begun would now, in daylight, seem daunting to her. I found myself concentrating, not on the hopeful interpretation of our somewhat ambiguous parting, but on its lack of commitment. And then I was assailed by self-doubt. Which led me back to my former wife and her assurances that my prospects outside our marriage were dim to nonexistent. You could bed the world on a one-shot basis, but something permanent, day-to-day? Only she had been mad enough to make that attempt, and now that she was all better . . . Well, there was probably no one left alive who would put up with the craziness she had endured these many years.

Yes, I know. It runs counter to the commonest of common wisdom, which holds that for every man there's a woman; runs counter to my own best sense of myself, which is that though I may not be the easiest person to live with, no one is, and that I am not without interest, even some rather adorable qualities once you get to know me.

And yet . . . And yet. Statistically speaking, I was indeed a washout. 0 for 1. .000 in the big game. Many strike-outs and only a few scratch singles, nothing out of the infield, really, to show for the long career that had preceded our final extra-inning encounter. I was still the picture of confidence as I strode to the plate, swishing a couple of bats, briskly pounding the dirt from my spikes before assuming a properly menacing stance in the batter's box. But I had convinced myself I couldn't hit a curve, that they could always get me out with some well-assorted junk. And around the league they knew it. Elizabeth might be a rookie, but she was canny, knew the book on me as well as anyone. Why shouldn't she breeze a few past me and send me muttering back to the dugout? Or, presuming she conceived of us as teammates, why should she make any permanent commitment to me, knowing full well the management would shortly be sending me back down to the minors for further seasoning?

Block that metaphor! I rose, carried my paltry pile of dishes to the kitchen sink, and headed for the bathroom and a calming shower. I was under it, alternately freezing and scalding, and not being calmed at all, thanks to a plumbing system of a spectacularly erratic nature, when the phone jangled again.

Would that I could resist its importunings, but that has always been impossible for me. It is a sign of my fundamentally optimistic nature. I never think that it is a creditor calling. Always I believe that it is going to be some stranger offering me an African safari, or at the very least, the opportunity to make a great deal of unexpected money. Or, this morning, that it was Elizabeth. I stepped from the shower, grabbed a large towel and dripped my way back to the living room.

Much crackle greeted me, then the voice of an Englishwoman, cheerfully brisk, then, at last, Denis Crabbe, co-producer of the special we were doing in England. Having to mind their shillings and pence these days, and having in any event only the wariest of relationships with the conveniences of our age (think how many of them still refer to the radio as the wireless), the English, on the phone, come on even more clipped than national custom normally dictates—especially transatlantic. After a moment, however, I realized Denis was further encumbered because he was trying to talk with an upper lip stiffened against incipient disaster.

The details are a bore, totaling to a typical show-biz catastrophe. What it came down to was that after a year of the most exhausting fiddle, his company and mine had arranged a two-hour "tribute" to the most Lordly of the English acting Sirs, which was also a kind of potted history of their theater and ours over the half century he had been acting—the assembled big guns of the English stage firing off tributes to their colleague and, best of all, doing some of his favorite scenes. Now what Denis was telling me was that the only slightly lesser Sir who had agreed to act as master of these revels was down with phlebitis, had been ordered to bed for the duration, and had to be replaced.

Denis had found an adequately titled substitute, who was not quite such a big name in the U.S. and would have to be approved by our American network. Next, and more formidable, my script would have to be almost completely rewritten. It had been tailored to our previous star and was very chatty and personal in tone. Now I would have to go through his replacement's history, seeking the telling anecdote, yesteryear's graceful *bon mot.* That meant going to London to dredge his memory. And then we would have to find a couple of scenes for him to do, and put all his intros into his own idiom, and . . . and . . . and.

"In other words, I'd better leave tomorrow."

"Tonight would be better," said Denis. "Actually, I've booked you on the BA flight at ten. Can you get to your people at NBC today?"

"Probably. The trouble is my other shows—especially the one I'm editing here. It needs me right now."

"I see. Well, then . . ."

"Never mind. I'll work it all out. Find me a place to stay and expect me tomorrow. I'll cable only in case of total disaster."

"Right-o, chum."

"Pip-pip," I said.

"Chin-chin," he said. Never Wodehouse with a limey; they'll always top you.

I sat for a moment with the phone in my hand, mentally ordering priorities to the tune of the dial tone. Then I turned into a blur.

Ten

Some eleven hours later, somewhere north of Boston at thirty thousand feet, the blur ceased to vibrate, began to resolve itself, once again, into a shape closely resembling that of a middle-aged human male. The process was rather like that of a character actor passing back through the rays of the machine that had dematerialized him in one of the earlier reels of a cheapish sci-fi movie. Or so I saw it in imagination.

Doubtless an objective observer would have found my transformation to and from the workaholic state less melodramatic. Though it did seem to me I had been the recipient of some rather odd looks as, prior to boarding, I had presented my hand baggage for inspection and passed through the metal detector. Disheveled, sweaty, still wild-eyed from fear that I would miss my flight, I imagined I quite closely resembled the hijacker profile airport security people are supposed to carry in their minds. Still, they had passed me through, and the hostesses had sold me headset and cocktail without so much as a rivet in the armor of their indifference coming loose. The only profile I apparently matched was the familiar one of the tired businessman.

It was, of course, an impenetrable disguise. Who on that nearly empty flight would know that the rumpled figure solemnly attempting to choke down a few bits of dusty chicken in seat 11–A (with sprawling privileges on B and C) was, in fact, the legendary international roué and womanizer David Koerner? To be sure, he might for the moment look like one of those small-time traders who work the Balkans in Eric Ambler's stories, but give him a change of clothes, a shave and a shine, place him in his proper context—Park Lane or Belgravia—and he assumes his true proportions, his witty, sophisticated, shrewd mind masked by an indolent air, but for all that romantic, even capable of sentiment . . . a character Noel Coward might have been pleased to create. You bet.

Let's put the matter as simply as possible: I really don't like transitions very much (which is one of the reasons I was such a bad sport about divorce), and manage them best, if at all, in slow motion. I won't deny I was grateful for the necessity to travel, to keep moving, during those first months of separation. It minimized opportunities for brooding. But rootedness is really my thing. Jerk me untimely from what I think of as a familiar, comfortable situation and I come all over funny.

Staring into the rapidly congealing remains of dinner, I reviewed the day's events, trying to impose some logical pattern on them. From that bed to this chair—who, really, was he who had made that journey? If, as the man says, action is character, then what character do we divine from David Koerner's actions this fine day?

Well, let's see. He got word to the network about his little problem and arranged a meeting for four that afternoon. In the interim he managed to pick up his shirts from the Chinaman and his suit from the cleaner, and to get his socks and undies in and out of the laundromat.

Whereupon he raced to the editing room he, or rather the corporation he maintained as a weapon in his endless, losing war with the IRS, rented deep in the dreary reaches of the West Fifties. Films are bought and sold—that is to say, talked about—in much more glamorous precincts. But all over the world the real work on them is done, by independent producers anyway, in dismal districts where rents are low and any amenity beyond a water cooler is regarded as a first step toward bankruptcy. Here cigarette butts were ground out, never to be swept up, on fraying wooden floors, and the windows were coated with impenetrable layers of grime, so the weather outside appeared always to be threatening.

Here my patient cutters, both young women, toiled uncomplainingly, often without adequate knowledge of my intentions, since I was forever elsewhere. Today my feverish energy had galvanized them, or maybe they were just glad to see their absentee landlord on the premises for a change. Anyway, there are moments in film-making that are entirely unlike any I've experienced elsewhere, when somehow a small group of people start anticipating one another's ideas, improving on them even before they are fully articulated. Then fingers fly across the editing machine, the cursing that usually accompanies a search through the trim barrels for an out you suddenly know must be an in takes on a humorous cast, and impatience with the director—in this case, me—for not shooting enough protective material is tinged with a certain wry affection for the brute, whose incompetence is now seen to be not entirely irredeemable. When these privileged moments occur—usually at some desperately inconvenient time—they blot everything else out, lifting you up out of your fretful dailiness, banishing anxieties about yesterday's mistakes and tomorrow's inevitable troubles. There is only the here and now: these dear friends and colleagues; this room, miraculously transformed into a temple of light; this film, suddenly an ingenious and inspiring example of man's creative powers.

The human instinct is to extend time of this quality as far as you can. Some part of my marriage had been lost in rooms like these, at times like these. Given a choice, I think now that I would have preferred not to know about them, would have preferred an emotionally steadier kind of work. But I had no choice; once you've experienced that elation, you helplessly keep seeking it anew.

Today the cost was small. I was late, by almost half an hour, to my network meeting. But I carried my little high-pressure system with me in the cab across town, became, as it were, a pleasant, restorative zephyr, breezing into that conference room, whisking the impatient frowns from the assembled faces, blowing the cloud of anxiety that had been building and billowing there right out to sea. By the time I was done, the network guys and the ad men were convinced that a divine providence had ordered up, strictly for their benefit, our former principal's medical misfortune, allowing us, in our admittedly late-blooming wisdom (I passed rather quickly over that point), to make the substitution now proposed. Ah, the wit, the grace, the warmth we were gaining—at no loss of time, therefore at no loss of money. In my personal series of great performances, that was one of the masterworks.

Less than an hour later, I was wafted on the wings of my own eloquence to my office—very Sam Spade-ish—on Seventh Avenue, where faithful Nora, my secretary, laid before me tickets, a teletyped confirmation of a hotel reservation, and a draft on our London bank (for expenses). A few inconsequential phone calls were placed, canceling lunch dates, stalling a couple of potential clients (for industrial films, ugh)—warm-up tosses, preparing me for a couple of high hard ones I had no choice but to fire.

The first of these was to Mort in L.A. There was a school of thought among my friends which said that, having lost my wife, I had deliberately taken on Mort as a temporary partner because I had this deep unconscious need for a jealous nag in my life. This, of course, is an example of wrong thinking. Nevertheless, I knew, and dreaded, Mort's response to the news that I would be delaying my return to his side for something over a month. He would yell and scream a lot. Which he did. For fifteen harrowing minutes. By the end of which time, having discharged all his accumulated anxieties, he felt fine and I felt as if the Seven Dwarfs had transferred their mining operations to the pit of my stomach.

And there was still one more phone call to be made. To my children, who must be told that Daddy would not be around to take them out next Sunday. Or the next. Or the next. Or the . . .

Carrie, who was impatiently nearing thirteen, would not be disappointed. At least she would not show it if she was, cool being her only absolute value. But Amy, nine, was quite another case. Amy, nine, was a dagger in my heart. When people asked me how the kids were "taking it," my replies had until recently been easy and confident. The girls were full of cheer when I saw them, especially Amy, who, unlike the rest of the family (stretching back through the couple of generations I knew on both sides), was entirely unguarded about her emotions. One time when she was not expecting me, I rounded the corner into our street and saw her playing in front of the house. Glancing up, she saw me and expressed her pleasure in exactly the stylized manner of a cartoon character—by jumping straight up into the air. As she raced toward me, you could almost see spurting from her heels those little conventionalized puffs of dust cartoonists employ to emphasize rapid movement.

But when she hurled herself into my arms, she also seemed to try to burrow into me—a small animal in need of some nourishment only I could provide, and, it seemed, did not provide enough of. There were other disquieting signs, too. Her teachers reported something like complete chaos in her work, a near total inability to remember assignment details and deadlines, a distracted air in the classroom; that sort of thing.

Gentle probing revealed that her cheerfulness was, in fact, a desperate performance. She figured my response to exile from the family must be what hers would have been—a feeling of isolation and abandonment—and so she sought always to be a source of reassurance and encouragement for me. She was not far wrong, God knows, but the strain of this self-imposed responsibility for my mental health must have been awful for a little kid. Worse, I discovered that she was riven by all the fears you'd expect a nine-year-old to have: that she would be afflicted with some strange, cruel stepfather or stepmother; that her mother's occasional threats of removal to Nome, Alaska, or possibly Teaneck, New Jersey (in Amy's mind, equidistant from New York), would be carried out and she would never see me again. Or perhaps her suddenly peripatetic father would fly off on one of his business trips never to return. You can see why, to one oppressed by these burdens, next week's assignment in Language Arts would be small potatoes. Or maybe she was using all her energies trying to wish reconciliation on Mommy and Daddy, leaving nothing over for school. Or maybe she was just in plain, old-fashioned pain, and it was blotting out all other considerations.

Whatever. You can see why I delayed this call, why I was relieved to hear Carrie's hello when I finally put it through. "Oh, fine," was the state of her being. "Lucky," was her response to news of my trip. "Will you be back in time for our play?" was her only concern, easily eased after I glanced at my desk calendar.

"I'm sorry I have to go," I said. "I'll miss you, baby." "Same here," she said. "I'll bring you a fabulous present," I said. "A postcard you could send me," she said, lapsing into an imitation of some comedian's imitation of his Jewish mother. I laughed. Her set had lately discovered The Joke and their collectors' zeal somehow freshened the stale chestnuts they treasured.

I asked for Amy, and was rewarded with a hesitant voice. "Dad? You going somewhere, Dad?"

"To London. To see the Queen."

"How long?"

"Not too long; a couple of weeks," I lied.

"You're always going away," she said.

"You could look at it another way; I'm always coming back."

"I miss you."

"I miss *you.*"

We were silent for a moment. "Amy," I said, "I love you a lot."

"I love you, Dad."

Someone had lately told me that reassurances ring false to kids if you don't share some of your pain with them, too. They get to thinking you're some kind of monster for being so goddam cheerful all the time. And then they feel they're utterly alone, isolated with a grief no one else seems to be sharing.

So I said: "Listen, Amy. Sometimes when I'm traveling I see some family all together doing something very simple— maybe just eating ice cream cones—and then I just ache for you guys."

There was a sniffle at the other end of the line.

"I didn't say that to make you sad," I said quickly. "I mean, sure, it makes me miss you for a minute. But then I think of all the good times we've had, and the good times we're gonna have. And I feel close to you and Carrie—you know, sort of connected even though we're apart."

"Yes?" Very dubious.

"Yes. Really, really."

"But I want to *see* you, Daddy."

"Me too, you. And it's going to be better. See, I'm finishing the show in London this trip. Then in a couple of months the one in Los Angeles'll be over. We'll have more time. . . ."

Promises, Promises. I'd been making them for years. And meaning them. And breaking them. Still, this time anyway, they seemed to comfort Amy, perhaps because they were familiar ground. Canny child, she shifted the conversation to things she wanted to do when I returned: A day in Chinatown was very much on her mind. And I still hadn't taken her to *Pippin.* And some divorced daddy had taken one of her friends for a whole weekend at Mystic Seaport in Connecticut. I suppose one of the small benefits of the rising divorce rate is that being the child of what we used quaintly to refer to as "a broken home" no longer marks you as a freak and pariah. On the contrary, it admits you to the latest kid underground, where tips on what to talk Daddy into doing during "visitation" (formerly, as we know, an occupation reserved to real ghosts, no reference intended to males who merely feel like spooks haunting the remnants of their former lives) are eagerly traded about.

Anyway, we concluded on an optimistic note and I hurled myself forth again—back to the cutting room to clean up details, home to the packing, with but the briefest pause for Gelusil and a lovely Cup-a-Soup; and then it was time for the cab to Kennedy, the ride made the more thrilling by a vehicle of spectatular decrepitude. One might expect to find such a taxi in the provincial capital of some banana republic, but it was preposterous and depressing in the Big Apple. The sullen, long-haired youth at the controls, however, fit right in. He fancied himself superior to his work, but did not quite know how to find the airport.

And so, here I was. The movie, which I had seen, came on. I donned earphones, switched to the classical channel and was rewarded with some lovely, soaring music—Russianate and romantic, and most suitable to sailing along in an airship, the moon casting a pale light on tattered clouds below, the ocean simply a blackness far below them. It was a very nice setting for an identity crisis, and I settled back to enjoy mine to the fullest.

Who was he, finally, this daring old man in his flying machine? A devoted father, surely, but often lax in his devotions. At work, Frank Cowperwood *manqué*. But also: absent friend, distracted lover, failed husband. And: self-appreciator, self-doubter, last angry man, escape artist. A convenience-food addict, trying to hurry through life's graceful moments because fearful of the silence of a civilized pause. A twentieth-century character in search of a nineteenth-century author. All of the above, none of the above.

One thing was certain, though. He was hardly the lover of

any woman's dreams. For surely a singular omission will have been perceived in this accounting of the day's activities: namely, the sparing of a thought for Elizabeth Adderley. Actually, I did try to reach her, from a pay phone in the RCA Building lobby. She was "not at her desk." A little later I tried again, from my office. By that time the receptionist at her place had gone home and after many rings an irritable male voice answered and informed me shortly that everyone had gone home. "Any message?" he inquired crossly, and the dictates of discretion aside, the impossibility of paring down what I had to say to something he could impatiently fit on his memo pad defeated me. "No. Thank you very much," I said. "I'll reach her tomorrow." I then requested that Nora call Elizabeth next day, tell her what had so suddenly become of me and to expect a letter.

But I was too tired to write just now, I thought, so I unplugged myself from the music, folded back armrests, gathered up the dolly pillows from the adjoining empty seats, arranged them between head and window, stretched out and began the search for some position in which sleep might have a chance to overcome discomfort. Over the next half hour I actually discovered a couple that were promising. But it was no use, for I was dealing, once again, with my "dirty little secret," the deepest source of such guilt as I harbored over the breakup of my marriage, the breakdown of sundry other relationships.

My trouble is that I love tight schedules and tight spots—days, weeks, in which my consciousness is entirely absorbed by the business of fitting too many appointments into too small a space, by the emotionless, but often thrilling, dramas of suspense I enact within the tight-printed lines of my desk diary. I love being brilliant under pressure, against deadlines. The daring leap, the flashy save—they are specialties of the house. Preoccupied by them, I have a perfect excuse for not attending to my emotions or to those that have been left in my care by people whom I have led—misled—to trust me. Eventually, of course, everyone stops believing my excuses for absence, impatience gives way to anger as they wait around for me on the street corners of the soul, and finally they just leave. Which, of course, provides me with a new motive for throwing myself still more maniacally into my work.

I am—or was—afraid of intimacy, afraid that my small gift for it would be used up, and that lacking the capacity to replenish it, I must hoard it like a miser. And, at the same time, give the appearance of generosity, lest the world discover that I was afflicted with this apparently congenital defect.

So, protesting love and longing, I had probably been as much in flight on the ground as I now was in the air. Once again love—more accurately, the possibility of love—had been driven out in favor of more manageable matters—work, career, ambition, whatever.

Except. Except I could not sleep. Perched there on my aluminum dot in space, hurtling anonymously through this trackless sky, over this trackless ocean, I knew a terrible anxiety. No, call it by its rightful name, which is dread. A terrible dread. I was literally in the middle of nowhere. Amy aside, of course, no one was saddened by my departure and, unless you counted Denis, which was preposterous, no one was anticipating my arrival. The Flying Fool, Nomad of the Jet Streams. And, at that, the worst kind of fool—a sad fool, maybe even a crazed fool. For is it not the very definition of madness to know that what you are doing is bound to do you harm and then go ahead and do it anyway?

Once, on another transatlantic flight, I had sat next to a man who literally had no home. As a sop to people who make up forms, he listed his daughter's split-level in suburban Philadelphia as his address, paying her a small sum to forward his mail and to keep the guest room open for him as an occasional resting place. "The Diners Club has to send your bills somewhere," he had said, "but I try to keep out of her way; just drop in three or four times a year." He had paused thoughtfully, then added: "Nice to see the grandchildren, of course."

In the months since I had encountered him, this nameless fellow had come to seem a cautionary figure to me. He was a wayfarer of the night, which is when he always tried to travel, he told me, sleeping on planes to save on hotel bills: "It adds up; thirty, forty nights a year—figure it out." He was also a connoisseur of cheap accommodations: "Domestically, you can't beat your TraveLodge." And a genius of cut-rate air travel: "You gotta think beyond Icelandic; you take these London show tours, now. . . ."

A gray man—gray eyes, gray hair, gray complexion, even a grayish suit and a grayish voice, guarded and thus without singularity of tone. Fittingly, he dealt in government surplus, bureaucracy's unemotional castoffs, a connectionless man who had achieved total mastery in the art of surviving without recourse to those life-support systems—family, communal, corporate—the rest of us consider essential to survival; a man living in the interstices of our civilization, never getting tangled in the webbing that links the rest of us together; a man avoiding the inconvenience of emotion, of loyalty, of love. As I was tempted to do.

It would not be hard. Laziness, fear of self-exposure, fear of some nameless hurt, the workings of some psychological birth defect—they all compelled one toward the peaceful, featureless antisepsis of the TraveLodge. One could find it without half trying. In fact, half trying was exactly the way to do it.

The vision of my one-time seatmate slowly faded, to be replaced by another image—of Elizabeth, stretched out by my side sleeping, unguarded and vulnerable, and (so it seemed) requiring no more than answering vulnerability from me. She was old friend as well as new lover. If I could not open myself to her, trust her, who else was there? No one, came the answer. So for chrissake try, I advised myself. And so I sat up, snapped on my reading light and pushed the call button.

A steward appeared.

"Sir?"

"Do you have some stationery?"

Eleven

This is what I wrote to Elizabeth:

My Dearest E,

By this time I hope you've received, via secretary bird, news of my sudden departure. I imagine no further explanation is required; as you know, my life now is full of sudden comings and goings. Anyway, such modest claims as we have on one another surely do not extend to obligatory reports on these matters. I hope they never will, freedom from such accountings being one of the great pleasures of the single life.

Still, as this is to be an extended trip, with a further absence in Los Angeles looming immediately after, I thought I ought to add something to the bare information you've been given.

God, those are stiff paragraphs. I feel suddenly shy, I guess, and I am long out of practice in writing what I daresay must be regarded as a love letter. Is the term too strong? Should I call this a fondness letter? No, that's silly. Well, certainly it is not a business letter.

What I want to say is that I regard what happened between us last night as a consequential act, even though neither of us knows just what its consequences will be. Old-fashioned fellow that I am, I do not take the act of love lightly—whatever I may seem to imply when us guys are joshing around in the locker room. I think there must—there ought to be—some sort of future for us. Anyway, I want there to be. Very much.

That paragraph at least has the virtue of not being dull. But it is, I'm sure, dangerous. I perceive in you a wariness, a skittishness in regard to any emotional commitment—and most especially one between us. Prudent, practical woman that you are, I imagine that the difficulties of pursuing an affair with me may well not seem worth the troubles involved. I mean, it's just not done, is it?—not when you may at any moment encounter Marion at the Shopwell, not while bonds of affectionate memory tie both our families together. It would be so much easier to dismiss our encounter of twenty-four hours ago as just one of those things (a trip to the moon on not quite gossamer wings). I share your doubts. In the end I think the history we already share will rise up to defeat the possibility of adding many new chapters to that history. I just don't foresee permanent or even exclusive arrangement between us.

But I must quickly add that, even so, I want to go on seeing you as often as I can for as long as I can. I can't reduce to the logic of grammar all the reasons behind that powerful compulsion. Much flowery writing would result. And much embarrassment—to both of us—would flow from that. This much I could perhaps risk:

I have, since leaving Marion's bed and board, busied myself almost maniacally, both professionally and romantically. That's been a matter of pride for me: not to show that I was hurting, or even especially unhappy. But I have been. Mostly, I've felt what I gather most people feel when their marriages bust up—betrayed. I felt betrayed by Marion, naturally, and betrayed by myself. When I'm thinking reasonably about the whole thing, I believe she made a completely moral decision (by her lights) when she asked me to leave. She really could not see any other alternative, though I must believe there were such. I also know that despite my protestations of shock, anger and general distress, there are moments when I am washed with this huge sense of relief—about which I feel no guilt at all. I expect you felt a similar mixture of emotions when Hilton upped stakes.

Still. Still and all. One has been partner to a failure. And it is of the kind that can only be described as a failure of trust. Since that failure I have found it difficult—no, impossible—to trust anyone again . . . not with my heart. And I include myself in that statement. That branch of the business has for some time been closed for alterations.

But I need to trust. Everyone does. And I need to prove myself once again trustworthy. I'm guessing it's the same with you, and that out of that coincidence, and our congruences of age and experience, not to mention old-friendship, we might make something good and valuable together. In the long run we may not continue to share the benefits of the kind of renewal I'm talking about, but I do know that together or separately we both need it.

I hope that all doesn't sound too abstract, like a lecture from a shrink or from an old college psych course. For—chaotically —there is much else on my mind. The sound of sleep in your voice, for example, the softness of your touch, the smoothness of your skin, the appraising look in your eyes giving way to humor or to sympathy, the toughness of your mind and its quickness—and the way those qualities mix so entrancingly with its tenderness. Some of these I had noticed as we glanced off each other in times past, but now, beginning to experience them with a new awareness, I want to know them much, much better.

But enough. You know what I'm trying to say—no need to overstress it. There is a faint smudge of gray visible on such of the horizon as I can see out the window, and a rattling up forward tells me the cabin crew is preparing the tea trolley so we can greet the dawn in proper English style. The turkey on the screen before me is about to gobble its last. So I will bring this to an end. Fear not, my lovely E. I will not try to possess you beyond my time. It's just that I don't want to leave before I have to. I hope you understand all I've been trying to say, and not say. I hope *I* understand.

All my love,

D

The steward, happening by, saw me trying to cram all that into the tiny airmail envelope he had provided earlier, and offered both to find a larger envelope and to post my effusion. Further inquiry determined that he was returning to the States next day and would be pleased to mail the letter there. Gratefully, I handed it to him and then, at last, a great exhaustion came over me and I slept—right through breakfast, as it turned out. Still, I was able to cadge a cup of tea from my friendly servant and to slurp it down as we passed over Land's End.

It was a glorious morning and I watched the hedgerows go by beneath. Even from a great height the trim tidiness of the English countryside is somehow conforting, so unlike the lonely vastness of the American earth. Our glide path into Heathrow was the glamorous one—straight up the Thames. Below, sunlight glinted on the comic spires of the Albert Bridge, that dear Victorian conceit. I remembered walking across it, on a fall day as perfect as this spring one, to sit on a bench in Battersea Park, to watch the late-afternoon light add its glow to that of the turning leaves, while a woman I loved, and have since lost, talked with me of that love's impossibility.

With her I had had my first, and only, extramarital affair. With her I began the process of reeducation in the good ways of women, in particular the sweet and patient indulgence they can offer a man they love, the idealism about the romantic impulse itself that they bring to bed with them. It was idealism, indeed, that brought our affair to an end that day. For she saw that all my talk to the contrary notwithstanding, I was not yet ready to give up on my marriage, and she was determined that our romance not contribute any more than it had to to the dissolution of the marriage. "It's a good thing," she had said, "and I don't want it used in a bad cause. Breaking up homes, especially when there are children involved, is a bad cause." There was irony in this. My wife did not discover the error of my ways until after this conversation had taken place, and her hurt and anger had been a sustaining force for her throughout our discussions of separation and afterward. On those rare occasions when her resolution wavered, Marion had but to remind herself of my betrayal in order to reheat and serve her angry leftovers. So, oddly, our affair had been used in the bad cause my good, dear friend had feared—but not by the party she had thought might use it.

As for us, we parted as lovers should, with gentle rue for what could not be, our memories unsullied by anger or re-crimination. I reviewed those memories now, as we made our final approach to the runway, and felt blessed by them. They seemed to me, like the fine weather I was about to step into, a happy omen.

And so they were, for things went well in London. I struck it off well with our new host, Sir Miles Poynter by name, and, for reasons of his own, he was of a mood for expansive reminiscence. He had a marvelous flat in Down Street—high ceilings; an Adam fireplace; a collection of antique glass paper weights mingling on the commodious coffee table with books he seemed actually to be reading; seascapes, landscapes and ancestor portraits (none of them his own, as he cheerfully informed me) artlessly crowding the walls. There we sprawled on couch and easy chairs, collaborating for a week of after-noons on his portion of the script, his manservant ever on call to provide refreshment.

His remembrances, together with the openness and unpre-tentiousness of his manner, brought forth from me anecdotes and reflections revealing more of my past history and present prospects than I would ordinarily have spilled before a stranger, especially in a situation where he was supposed to do the talking, I the listening. But he was—this precise, perhaps compulsive, actor—essentially a character man, collecting and hoarding, against his future theatrical needs, material he could draw on for possible roles. He was also, I learned, a man who insisted on balanced exchanges. If he bought lunch one day, he wanted you to buy it the next; if he offered a revelation, he expected one in turn—not immediately, but before the day was done, surely. In bits and pieces, then, he got rather a complete picture of me, though I did not know that he was connecting these conversational dotted lines, coloring in the spaces they contained, creating for himself a detailed portrait of me, until early the following week.

I arrived late and fuming for one of our appointments, delayed by some nonsense at the office. I tried to cover a harassed air with apologies, but Miles was having none of that. Instead, he decreed that we take the afternoon off, and since the day was fine, he proposed a stroll through the Green Park to end up at White's, his club in St. James's, for a drink. I was glad to accept, and as we meandered along, my new friend launched into a monologue about his middle years, when success had belatedly come to him, with what he described as a terrifying suddenness. After so many thin years, he wanted all of it, every last magazine interview and benefit performance. A marriage got mislaid and he felt the edge of his talent dulling through overuse, and there were unspecified "psychologic" troubles. Then, however, he was overpaid for a job in Hollywood, met a woman there who seemed worth pausing for, and they escaped for half a year, to a pleasant succession of islands in the South Pacific. He had, he said, regained his perspective during that pause. Now he was urging a similar respite on me.

I agreed in theory, but in practice I pointed out that my Hollywood offers precluded any vacation more elaborate than a weekend in Tijuana. "Oh, make it Santa Barbara," he said.

"Come on," he added, "I'm not thirsty yet. Let's go play with the pelicans," and so saying, angled off on one of the walks leading toward the pond in St. James's Park, where the more exotic waterfowl of the realm are spoiled rotten by dotty old ladies. Then, on a bench there, a late-afternoon chill settling around us, he turned his famously compelling gaze on me and reverted to his previous theme: "If you won't take six months, I wish you'd take six days," he said.

"What?"

"When you've finished the script, just before we record, you really ought to go away for a while—tour about, read some useless books. Then come back and look at the entire program: see what you think after you've stepped back from it a bit."

"It's a good idea."

"I have a little cottage. It's in a village in the West Country, not two hours from here. I shan't be using it the remainder of this month."

"Oh, I couldn't. . . ."

"Nonsense, my dear boy. Of course you could."

"It's very kind of you."

"Nothing of the sort. It's completely in my own interest. More than one playwright has written a splendid second-act curtain for me there."

"It's awfully tempting."

"A long weekend. And, if you have a friend . . ."

Thus did this kindly old gentleman change my life.

For the instant he spoke that last sentence, I knew what I was going to do. Or try to do. I simply asked him if I could have a few days to try to arrange things before making a definite commitment, then as quickly as possible steered him back to White's, refused his offer of a second drink, and set off briskly down Piccadilly toward our office, a plan buzzing insistently in my brain, my pulse thumping loud and fast.

We are, most of us, cultural laggards with regard to long-distance travel. For hundreds of years, after all, the crossing of oceans and frontiers was a weighty thing, involving extensive preparations, weeks in transit, the thrill of adventure and, at the same time, an exile's anxiousness, all of which require large emotional expenditures. And so we still tend, even those of us who travel to excess, to think we are farther from home, more profoundly out of touch, than we actually are. London was, for example, just six and a half hours and a few hundred dollars from New York. And, if she was willing to invent them, just a couple of excuses for Elizabeth. Indeed, striding along, I made them up for her.

It made such marvelous sense to me. We might never get to know each other if we kept meeting on the fly, on the sly, in New York. But give us a time out of time, a time that belonged to us exclusively, in which we could create a little place of our own, free of responsibility's intrusions, free of associations that would awaken the play of memory, why, then . . .

Why, then, anything was possible. And if things did not work out for us, we would at least know that we had given ourselves a good chance. And taken exclusive possession of a memory in which we had shared creation with no one else.

The office was deserted by the time I arrived. But neatly centered on my desk there was a letter addressed to me in a hand I did not recognize. The script was firm and functional; no nonsense about it. I guessed immediately who it was from, and this is what it said:

My Dear D,

I envy you England. It has been too many years since I was there. But I would probably envy you Weehawken, so tightly bound am I now to home and office—hard for a girl who is used to feeling that airlines had been established solely as a guarantee of instant escape every time a sinkful of dishes or a stopped-up drain was too much to bear.

I was grateful for your secretary's call, as I would surely

have tried to reach you in the next day or two and would have been obscurely resentful at discovering your whereabouts belatedly, surprisedly. How quickly we begin to assert claims on one another!

As for your letter, I don't know how you managed it. It bore an American stamp and it arrived just three days after you left. I presume you bribed someone to act as courier. You do know your way about the world, don't you? It is a nice quality, that competence, and having been associated with a man who could never get a long-distance call through on the first try, I admire it, perhaps more than I should.

As for what you had to say, it was almost as surprising as its arrival. I never imagined you having a handwriting at all. I thought all communication with you must involve a machine of some sort. To and froing past your house, when you kept an office there, I used to see you in your window, wreathed in cigarette smoke, either talking into your eternal phone or, as I once thought, trying to warm your hands, against what cold I can now begin to imagine, over your typewriter.

That all seemed to suit you—the busywork, the tension. You were never less than pleasant to me and mine. But never more than distracted, either. Sometimes, when I saw you with your children, I thought I caught a hint of something else. For want of a better word I called it generosity the other night. In bed with you I was not surprised to find it present—as I think I mentioned. What I didn't mention was its force, its all-encompassing force. I really didn't know how brilliantly you could mobilize that quality. It briefly swept me away.

Maybe that is a damaging admission, but in my not-so-limited experience, generosity (above and beyond the obligatory bunch of posies) is not so common as you might think, and I did love being its recipient.

You spoke in your letter about what happened between us as a "consequential act." I agree, but I think we probably define the term differently. I love the moment when a man and a woman shed clothes and inhibitions and join themselves, form a bond against encircling nothingness. That bond is now forged between us and, in my mind anyway, it is unbreakable. It has never seemed important how many times I renew that connection—once, twice, three times; it makes no difference to me. Because the important fact has already been established: a love has been created and it has a life of its own, in my mind and (I always hope) in his as well. Whether it has a large or small existence in the world of things and events is not important to me.

Now, I'm not trying to let you down gently. I do want to see you again. And expect to see you again. But you are right: I am afraid of what comes next. I am not afraid of what people might say if they found out (though obviously discretion is to be desired, mostly because I have always enjoyed being discreet about my doings, not sharing them with the entire bridge club). What I'm afraid of is, once again, your generosity. It's as I said the other night. I want to be free for a while, unencumbered, unentangled—and I think you might be able to rob me of that privilege. For there is a strength in your capacity for giving that could, I fear, overpower (as they used to say in old-fashioned novels) a poor, weak woman such as me.

I hope that doesn't sound impossibly confused, paradoxical. I guess what I'm trying to say is really very simple: use me gently, dear D.

And now I must go—to bed. To a lonelier bed, I must admit, than it has up to now been. I wish you success in all your endeavors (it should be endeavours, shouldn't it?) over there, and much happiness, too. I'd love it if you'd write again, if you have the chance. Especially in longhand.

Your loving,

E

I held the letter in my hand for some time after reading it, then reread portions of it, as if I were a literary critic subjecting them to close textual analysis. I decided that I loved the letter. I decided that I hated the letter.

What I loved about it should be obvious. After all my gloomy speculations regarding my tragically flawed character, it was good to discover that a woman of obvious sensitivity and perspicacity valued the very qualities I was certain I lacked.

What I hated in it was its reserve, its caution, as, thinking back, I hated those qualities in my own letter. I did not expect, would not have known what to do with, a confession of consuming passion. It is not that people over forty are incapable of such declarations. Quite the opposite: they are more than ever a necessity. It is just that a degree of circumspection was to be expected among us. Suited us, actually. We had not lived that long for nothing—or so we must believe in consolation for the step or two we have lost in moving from baseline to net. Canniness will, we are forced to believe, compensate for our still minor infirmities of physique and spirit.

But. Shit. Granting all that, had we not the right now and then to throw caution to the winds, to grab what was never granted adults without a fight: namely, time of your own, time to which you could impart a special shape and distinction? Time that could just possibly exert a changing force on the rest of your life, but which at least would not be lost when it mingled with all the other moments as they were carried down the stream of years.

I thought that Elizabeth had not been thinking about time of that quality much lately. No more had I. Well, thanks to Sir Miles, I was in a position, suddenly, to make a gift of time to both of us. It required only the will to selfishness to accept it, and I never had understood why the exercise of that quality should be the exclusive prerogative of the young.

Elizabeth had led a responsible life, I had led a responsible life. All our children had had twice-yearly dental checkups, both of us had faithfully attended conferences with their teachers, I grudgingly carried life insurance, she made certain her family each day ingested the minimum daily requirement of all the stuff they list on the sides of cereal boxes, we both maintained a faithful watch for cancer's seven danger signals. Lawyers, accountants and the *Cue* restaurant guide were consulted on all appropriate occasions. Summers at camp and winters with flute teachers were arranged for the kids, as requested. Should we detect one of their psyches going ta-pocketa, ta-pocketa, it would be driven forthwith to a psychiatric grease monkey for repairs—and so what if that meant skulking around for another winter clad in the pallor of the Manhattan minimum-security prison while all about us were turning toasty brown in St. Thomas.

Well, goddammit, enough was enough. I wanted her. And I wanted time together for both of us. It was as simple as that. And if her need for me was not as urgent, there was no doubting her interest. Let her for once, let me for once, not concern ourselves with "what comes next." Let us, in fact, determine for ourselves, without reference to anyone else's interests or opinions, what should come next. Just once. Just for a little while.

And besides, who can resist England now that April's here?

I was not myself—quite deliberately not my self-doubting, self-analyzing self—as I grabbed up the phone, got the overseas operator and reached Elizabeth at her office.

"Yes?" Her voice was hesitant, and distance made it seem small.

"Goddammit, Elizabeth," I greeted her, "this is David. Now listen to me. And don't say yes until I finish talking."

Twelve

The crowd at Terminal Three—the international building at Heathrow—numbered, as it always seems to, several hundred. They were pressing, politely yet firmly, against a barrier that prevented them from spilling into the customs area but gave them a view of passengers as they debouched, trundling their luggage on trolleys, some of them staggering slightly under the impress of jet lag, through customs' sole exit.

The arrival board chattered and a line of letters and digits thereon spun madly, announcing that Elizabeth's plane had landed just as I entered this scene. There was no hope of working my way to the front of the crowd, and so I took my place at the end of the short passageway formed by the barrier, at that point where passengers were obliged to abandon their last vestiges of special status, rejoining the rest of struggling humanity in the search for that prosaic yet elusive convenience, ground transportation.

Things were aroil here, some travelers breaking into glad cries as they spotted loved ones, others bustling offstage with a great, doubtless false, air of knowing what they were doing. Still others stood stock still, momentarily paralyzed by the necessity once again to make decisions for themselves after several hours when that capacity was abandoned in favor of the airlines' corporate wisdom. All in all, despite the confusion, I judged this to be the best available vantage point, especially since I contrived to station myself next to a guard whose business it was to make himself highly visible, thus highly accessible, to questioning strangers.

After all my dither, it had been surprisingly easy to persuade Elizabeth to make this trip. Circumstances, as it turned out, had been in our favor: her boss had been planning a business trip this week and had been glad to give her a week off—at no pay, since she had not worked for him long enough to be entitled to vacation. She had then simply informed her children that she must accompany him on his journey, which, she said, was to Tulsa. There resided a college roommate of exemplary trustworthiness. She agreed to tell the kids Mom was out should they call in sick or lonesome, then pass the message to my office in London, whence Elizabeth could direct-dial advice and sympathy.

Beyond hesitating a day while making these arrangements, she had never questioned the wisdom of my invitation. She would tell me later that she wouldn't have dared to, so forcefully had I blustered it. Besides which, as she rather inelegantly put it, she would have considered an invitation to San Clemente, so desperate was her need for a change. "It was an offer I couldn't refuse," she said, doing her excellent impression of Brando.

On the phone, we had kept things cool and light. You would have thought we were arranging nothing more complex than a weekend in the Hamptons. I had not, however, told her that I would meet her plane or where she would be staying, claiming difficulty in finding a suitable hotel room. I had asked her simply to meet me at the office. What I was planning, needless to say, was a grand gesture, an expensive, romantic surprise.

Now that was all laid on, and I was well pleased. But anxious. For if, somehow, we missed one another in the airport crush, a tired lady would be greatly inconvenienced and I would look a great fool. I was certain that I couldn't possibly miss her, but as time wore on, as literally hundreds of passengers swept past me, I began to doubt. And to try to keep the rest of this large and crowded room under surveillance, paying special heed to the *bureau du change*, the most popular immediate destination, which I couldn't keep in constant sight from the position I had chosen. Twice I observed tall, dark-haired women who, from the back, looked like Elizabeth—the second one so much so that I turned and took several steps in her direction, thinking to catch her up. Just then, though, I felt a hand on my arm and heard a familiar voice:

"Hello, David."

I turned. "I just happened to be passing by," I said.

We embraced and she pulled me tight to her, as if in need of reassurance. It surprised me, but it shouldn't have. She had come far and lied some in order to reach this moment. I encircled her in my arms and when we ceased to kiss she buried her face in my shoulder. "I'm awfully glad you're here," she said.

"Surprised?"

"Not really."

After a moment we stepped back from each other, but continued to hold hands. "You look fine," I said. "You must have got some sleep."

"Not a wink. I was like a kid. I didn't want to miss a thing, even when there was nothing to miss. What you're seeing is Christmas morning."

"Merry Christmas, Elizabeth."

"Same to you," she said, and planted a quick, happy kiss on the corner of my mouth.

I took over her baggage cart with one hand, and slipped my free arm around her waist, guiding her toward an exit.

"Don't I need to change some money?"

"You can do it at our bank. The rate should be a little better."

"It says taxis down there, to the left."

"I've got a shortcut," I said.

"Don't you ever get tired of being masterful?" she asked.

"That's the whole point. I almost never am. You seem to bring it out in me."

Outside, Charles was waiting. "I'll take that, sir." He lifted Elizabeth's two bags off the trolley and I said, "Thank you, Charles." Elizabeth looked wonderingly at me as the chauffeur opened the trunk—pardon me, boot—of the waiting Bentley.

"Holy Hannah," said Elizabeth.

"Just the beginning," I said.

"David!"

I grinned. "Actually, it belongs to our chairman. He lets us play with it occasionally."

I bundled her into the back seat, Charles hustled around to shut the door after us, and soon enough we were gliding through the airport's access roads, then out onto the M4.

"Where are you taking me?" Elizabeth asked, mock terror in her voice.

"There's this secluded manor house, known to but a few of the city's most notorious rakes."

"I knew it—*The Story of O*."

"In a moment I press a hidden switch, curtains roll down, and I shall have you completely in my power."

"You do, you know. In a funny way. I hadn't thought of that."

I laughed and squeezed her shoulder. "Why don't you just relax and watch the scenery? If I'm not mistaken, there's a very nice sign for Maclean's toothpaste coming up in a few minutes."

"I could use some. And a hot bath."

"Know the feeling. You could just close your eyes. The admirable Charles will see us safely home."

And she did, rousing herself once or twice to try to pry our destination out of me, but in such an uninsistent murmur that I was able to turn her questions aside with a "Shh," and some parental-like pats. Toward the end of the drive her head was resting sleepily on my shoulder.

The stops and starts imposed on us by traffic as we drew near the center of the city roused her, and as we circled Wellington's house at Hyde Park Corner I nodded and said, "They were booked."

"Are we near?"

"Yes."

She busied herself with comb and lipstick, seemingly much revived. "I'd forgotten," she said. "How soft the colors are —the greens and grays."

"How long has it been for you?"

"I was counting up. Ten years. A decade. It sounds so much more when you call it a decade. It was right after Annie was born. Hilton brought me along on one of his pretend business trips."

"Swinging London. Mostly I missed that phase."

"You didn't miss much."

Suddenly, she squealed. "Oh, my God, David. You're kidding."

"What?"

"Claridge's. We're stopping at Claridge's."

"Only place I could get a room." I spoke gruffly, wondering if perhaps I had overdone it.

"What's this costing you?"

"A lot less than you think. You said it yourself: I know my way around."

And that much was true. Hotels make special rates for people they think can do them good. TV and movie people, journalists—we often get cut-rate accommodations on the assumption—generally unwarranted, but never discouraged— that we will work the hotel's name into our copy sometime, somehow.

We were out of the car and inside the door, crossing the cavernous, gloomy lobby, another age's idea of impressive— which, by God, it was. "I've already checked us in," I said. "All I have to do is leave your passport with the head porter.

The lift is just here, to the left."

In a moment we were creakily ascending and a moment after that I was opening the door to our suite.

"It looks like a Noel Coward set," Elizabeth said.

"Just what I thought."

The living room held overstuffed sofas and chairs—blond wood inlaid with still lighter wood in geometric designs, the fabric brown and a little worn, but comfortably so—grouped around an electrified fireplace. The lamps, slender brass creations with fringed shades of a sort I recalled from childhood, were turned on and glowed pinkly. Facing the door was a large window with heavy drapes pulled back to let in the day's gray light. Before it stood a dining table. The flower-patterned rug, also nicely worn, was, I swear, an Aubusson.

Elizabeth passed through this room, touching things softly. "The ceiling," she said, "the ceiling." It was worth calling attention to—surely fourteen feet high, adorned by garlands of gilt, with a splendid chandelier dropping from its center.

"Bedroom's to the left," I said. She turned from the window and entered it. I followed.

She made as if to bounce on the bed, but that proved impossible. She sank into it instead.

"I hope you don't have lower-back problems," I said.

"Down?" she asked, touching the comforter, folded in a neat triangle at the foot of the bed.

"I imagine."

"Yum," she said, and flopped back on the bed. Once again it seemed to me I was seeing the girl she had once been, rather than the woman I had known so long. I started to move toward her, but there was a knock at the door: luggage arriving. When I had tipped the man, she opened the smaller bag, distributing things around the room—cosmetics to the dressing table, two paperbacks to the nightstand. The territorial imperative in action. I sat on the bed watching her. She caught the bemused look on my face and said, "Oh, the hell with it. I really want that bath."

"Shall I order anything? Coffee, tea?"

"Oh, yes. Tea would be lovely."

She headed for the bathroom and at the doorway gave a joyful yelp. "David! It's palatial!"

"It is rather, isn't it?"

"Grand hotels! How I've missed them."

She closed the door and turned the taps on full. I rang for the hall porter and ordered tea, which arrived while Elizabeth was still splashing about in the tub. I walked over to the window and stood staring out into the quiet street below. I felt suddenly shy; domesticity was a new mode—or was it a metaphor?—for us.

I said through the door: "Tea is served, madame."

"Oh," she replied, "I can't get out of the tub. Not yet. Would you bring me a cup?"

"How do you take it?"

"Milk, no sugar."

The bathroom was warm and steamy when I entered. She was stretched out full length in the enormous tub, the water pulled up under her chin as if it were a soapy blanket. She covered her breasts with one arm as she reached for the tea with the other.

I made to leave, but she said: "Why don't you bring yours in here? I was just beginning to feel lonesome."

I did as I was told, and seated myself on the little wooden stool the management had provided for such occasions. I didn't know what to say and I didn't know what to do with my eyes. I didn't want to seem to be staring at her, yet I didn't want to seem to be too obviously averting my gaze. I felt foolish.

She sensed that and grinned. "It's O.K., David. Modesty is not one of my virtues."

"It *is* one of mine, oddly enough."

"A true son of the middle border."

"Middle class, more likely. And then, of course, Marion and I spent a lot of time hiding from each other."

"Tolstoy was wrong. It's the unhappy families that are all alike."

"Yeah," I said. "Listen, do you want a schedule, or should I keep surprising you?"

"Just for today, surprises. But not too many of them."

"No. In fact, come to think of it, there aren't too many more. I figured you'd like a lot of space in the day."

"Yes." She finished her tea, and handed cup and saucer to me. I set it on the basin, then turned back to her, taking her left hand in my right. Looking down at her, I said: "I'm awfully glad to see you."

She said: "I'm awfully glad to be here."

She made to rise, and I pulled her up. Water streamed off her. Her dark skin glistened. There was a hollowness in my stomach and I couldn't seem to swallow. It is quite literal to say that my knees felt weak, a sensation I had felt only in fear, never in love.

I could not speak, so I reached for one of the towels, neatly stacked on a bench against the wall. Picking it up, I saw that it was not a towel at all, but a huge white terry-cloth robe. "Well, lookee here."

"Hot damn," she said.

I held the robe for her and she shrugged into it, then pulled it tight around her body, hugging herself for a moment. Then she took my hand and led me into the bedroom. There she turned to me and let the robe fall open in a gesture that was unaffected yet in no sense casual.

Thirteen

We slept. My exhaustion, the result of cramming a great deal of work into a few days in order to have time free for her, matched her jet lag. And truth to tell, anticipation had kept me up very late the night before and awakened me early that morning.

It was early afternoon before I stirred. Elizabeth was still asleep, resting on her side, legs drawn up, hands lightly clasped next to her face, which was turned away from me. Her breathing was deep and steady.

I kissed her lightly on her forehead, and slipped stealthily out of bed, making my way to the bathroom on tiptoe. I showered, and when I returned she opened one sleepy eye.

"Oh, that was marvelous," she said.

"Do you want to sleep some more?"

She considered. "No," she said. "I think I'm hungry." She paused for a moment, thinking things over, then said, "In fact, I *know* I am."

"Room service? Or would you like to get out into what's left of the day?"

"Out, please. A walk would feel good."

"Tea at the Ritz?"

"Are they still doing that?"

"Good as ever. Just like the changing of the guard."

"I did that once with my mother. The first time I ever came here. Do you know, she went out and bought me some white gloves to wear?"

"How old were you?"

"Twelve. I was being given the semi-grand tour. Mother kept being disappointed. It was right after the war, and all her memories were pocked with bomb sites."

"Were you disappointed?"

"No. It seemed to me I was stepping in and out of books I had read."

She rose and stretched and slipped out of her gown. "God, what a slob I've become. I didn't unpack a thing. Everything'll be wrinkled."

"What would Mother say?"

" 'How have I failed?' I imagine."

She clicked open her suitcases—well-worn Vuittons, very suitable to their present environment—and busied herself shaking out dresses, skirts, pants, inspecting them for travel damage, placing them just so on the hangers she found in the closet. We talked about details: what time we were picking up the rental car tomorrow, reconfirmation of her reservation home, neutral sorts of things. It was a way of catching our breath.

She pulled some panties, flower-printed, from her suitcase and as she bent to step into them, backlit by the light filtering softly through the curtains on the window, I thought—pretentiously—of Impressionist nudes. I said, "You're so beautiful."

She was silent, concentrating more than was strictly necessary on hooking her bra. "It's nice of you to say so," she said at length, "but I think you're crazy."

"You know I'm not."

"It's just . . . Oh, forget it."

97

"You're going to have to learn how to take a compliment again."

She looked up at me and smiled. "Yes," she said. "Yes, I really am."

I got out of bed, retrieved my clothes from the floor, where they had been scattered that morning, and started dressing. She brushed past me, on her way to the dressing table, and I caught her wrist, turned her to me, tipped her chin up and kissed her lightly.

"You really are an adorable man," she said.

And then it was my turn to protest. She cut me off in midsentence. "Shhh," she said, and placed a finger against my lips.

We quickly finished dressing, and descended to the lobby via the great broad staircase that swept in a grandiloquent curve down from the second floor.

"What an entrance," Elizabeth said.

"Too bad no one's looking," I said.

"But just as well. I hope London's not crawling with members of the Hawthorne PTA." Hawthorne was where both of my kids and one of hers went to school.

"Too early for them. They're all running around midtown earning money for the trip."

Outside, it had turned almost fair. There was far more blue than gray in the sky.

"Turner clouds," Elizabeth said as we strolled along.

"They always seem to move faster than ours," I said. "They're the only things here that do."

We came to a turning and a greensward beckoned to us.

"It's Berkeley Square, isn't it?" she said as we drew nearer.

"You've got a good memory."

"I was a very impressionable kid. And we walked a lot. It all seems to stay with me."

"Do you suppose it's an omen—Berkeley Square?"

"How do you mean?"

"Well, I'm not exactly a Browning, but you're at least an Elizabeth."

She took my hand as we strolled through the square. She was still holding it when we entered the Ritz.

I love the room where tea is served there: colonnades, mirrors, brocade, Louis XIV chairs, a genteel hubbub of sound. As usual, it was crowded, but we didn't have to wait long for a table. Elizabeth got to pour, and we demolished the little crustless tea sandwiches as if they were heroes and we were construction workers. But they give you a great pile of them, and when the pastry cart rolled around we chose modestly, passing up some multilayered concoctions of obviously disastrous caloric content.

As Elizabeth was nibbling the last of her peach tart, I said, "I just had a thought."

"Yes?"

"What I thought was that I haven't had a thought all day."

"It seems a shame to spoil the record."

"I suppose it's inevitable. But you know what I mean. I've given myself entirely over to sensation. The taste of this food, the light coming through the trees in the square." I paused. "The look of you. Your . . . perfume."

I turned away, suddenly embarrassed.

She touched my arm. "I *do* know what you mean. And it's lovely."

I looked at her. Questioningly. There was just the tiniest note of surprise—or maybe it was relief—in her tone.

"I almost didn't come. At the last minute."

"I thought that might happen. I stayed out of the office all day yesterday. So you couldn't reach me."

"Oh, I would have cabled, coward that I am."

"How come you didn't?"

"A bad reason. Hilton."

I waited for her to go on. "It was nothing, really. I was right in the middle of vacillating when he called. He'd made a date with Annie—his first in more than a month, by the way—and he was trying to get out of it. Something about having to work on the prospectus for his latest brainstorm. And his jogging. And his fucking, I suppose."

I laughed. "Now, Elizabeth. Fair's fair."

"Anyway, I said, Gee, that's too bad, because I have to go away for a week, and I was just wondering if he could spend some time with all the kids. Buy them a pizza or something over the weekend—just so they could see a parental face."

"And then the fun began."

"Do you know what he said, the creep? He said, 'Gosh, Libs, I think we're going to have to rethink this job of yours, if it's going to mean absenting yourself from the children on a regular basis.' That's an exact quote."

"It's sure an exact imitation," I said, admiring again that gift for mimicry, which come to think of it her sometime husband shared.

"Can you imagine! When I've been out of the house exactly one night since he left. Besides which, what does he think we're living on? I've had one check from him—for three hundred and seventy-five dollars—in four months."

I shook my head, all sympathy. And yet, such are the fault lines in divorce, so neatly do they follow the male-female division, that I felt a vagrant sympathy for poor Hilton. Sometimes there are occasions when you have no choice but to disappoint the children. Sometimes, even when there are no conflicting claims on your attention, you just can't face them, so poignantly do they remind you of what was, what might have been. Also, I envied him. Imagine getting off that lightly financially.

Elizabeth's mood was still fierce. "Anyway, I slammed down the phone and started packing my bags."

I smiled; rather distantly, I guess.

She touched my hand. "I'm sorry," she said. "Wrong tone for the Ritz."

"Hey, forget it. Anger's very useful for getting us from here to there. And since there is here in this case . . ."

"Yes." Now she squeezed my hand. "Look, let's make a deal. Let's not talk about our exes. Anyway, try hard not to."

"Shake," I said. And, solemnly, we shook hands.

"Of course, we'll break our word," I said.

"Naturally," she said, rising, taking my hand and pulling me toward the exit and further explorations of her remembered London.

Fourteen

I don't know why Virginia Woolf keeps intruding on this narrative. Maybe it's because she's on everybody's mind these days. The feminists keep trying to claim her, of course, though her life and work can't be captured within the thin metaphorical net they are always spreading. The rest of us are interested in her, I think, as a neurasthenic heroine—someone whose talent kept triumphing over her troubles, as we pray ours someday may. What everybody seems to avoid discussing is the steel in her, that tough shrewdness which gives strength to her work.

Anyway, Woolf talks, in one of her autobiographical fragments, about what she calls moments of being and non-being. The former are the stuff of memory, intense and shaping. But these, she says, are "embedded in many more moments of non-being . . . a kind of non-descript cotton wool."

Great writers, she thought, were capable of rendering both kinds of existence, but she modestly excluded herself from their number, and the rest of us must naturally follow suit. So in this accounting of a few days which contained more moments of being in a shorter span of time than I had ever experienced before, you must take it as a given that there were "many more"—many, many more—of those nondescript moments.

That night, for example, after we left the Ritz. We could not eat again for a while, and we could not sleep yet. That left drinking. Eventually our wanderings led us into Bond and Regent streets, and after studying the shopwindows, we found a pub in Conduit Street, one of the few in that area, which is not much frequented by the class of drinkers who enjoy public houses. "Do you like bitter?" I asked Elizabeth, as we penetrated the smoke and babble. "Do you know, I've never had it? Is it?" "Is it what?" "Bitter." "No, that's the point, it's about the mellowest drink I've ever tasted." And so she decided to try some, and she liked it, drinking on her feet, gently jostled by homeward-bound office workers lost in their own conviviality, the noise of which precluded conversation of more than fragmentary nature. Thus, Elizabeth's first taste of bitter—very nice, I'm sure, but not quite a Moment of Being, either.

After that, we drifted some more, even considered a movie we both felt we really ought to see. But the quotations from the critics, emblazoned on the theater's posters, were daunting: too many implicit moral imperatives in them. "Still," she said, "I'd like to go to a movie with you, just like I'm looking forward to having breakfast with you, and all the other little ordinary things." "How would you feel if I asked you to wash out my socks?" "About the same way you're going to feel about my panty hose hanging over the shower rod."

Finally, we returned to the hotel, ordered lamb chops and baked potatoes and profiteroles from room service—the former assuaging a sudden need for the basic and the familiar, the latter an act of self-conscious self-indulgence. We ate and then got ready for bed and then cuddled, amused at our own will to childishness, while watching an old Ealing comedy—not one of the famous ones, but full of those faces that were living caricatures of the English virtues, poking gentle fun, just by existing, at the commonly held values of a nation, such activity being, naturally, one of that nation's most enduring and endearing values. Both of us, as it happened, had been of an impressionable age when those Ealings had first invaded the American art houses and we had a high nostalgic regard for their foursquare artlessness. We murmured sleepily of that as the film approached its climax, she in her chaste nightie, I in my conservative pajamas, navy blue with white piping. Elizabeth was asleep, I think, before I switched off either telly or reading lamp, and I quickly followed. We lay close to one another. Once or twice during the night my breath stirred her hair and it tickled my nose. Once or twice I felt her breath on my cheek, and always there was the warmth of her presence.

Closeness of this kind had been a rarity in my life. Where I come from we don't touch much, and in marriage my wife and I had convinced one another that we were insomniacs, and after fitful experiments with the alternatives had early on fallen into the habit of staying well away from each other in our king-sized bed, each fearing the other's accusation of sleep-stealing. Eventually, as you can imagine, I became a genuine insomniac, a pill freak and worse, the prisoner of neurotic rituals designed to propitiate blessed Morpheus, the only god whose wrath I feared. Closet doors must all be closed before I tucked up; a glass of water and an assortment of reading material, suitable for differing nocturnal moods, must be present on my night table; bedclothes had to be folded back just so. Then it was necessary to read for a certain period of time—not too little, not too much—before snapping out the light. All that effort often as not failed to produce results, and 2 A.M. might find me in the living room, supplementing pills with booze and reading the most soporific literature available.

Marion claimed, quite rightly, that all this nonsense was anti-romantic, a distinct turnoff. On the other hand, it was her habit to undress behind an open closet door, fearful that a glimpse of breast or ass would turn me into a monster of sexual appetite, and she usually kept her underpants on under her nightgown, so that if it rode up during the night, nothing would be revealed that might awaken my ravening lusts. And it was true that I constantly desired her, for she is a handsome woman, tall, long-thighed, those closely guarded breasts just simply breath-taking to me when they were revealed.

Perhaps it was shrewd of her to continue playing the blushing bride a decade and more after we were married, familiarity never being allowed to breed ennui. But my insomnia, breeder of those rituals she found so off-putting, had, in turn, been bred by sexual frustration. To lie, night after night, next to a woman you adore, knowing from bitter experience that to reach out to her was to invite rebuff, would make a night owl of Rip Van Winkle. Those sleeping pills, generally swallowed simultaneously, so that (theoretically) we would simultaneously fall asleep, were, finally, a kind of unspoken suicide pact for our marriage.

So perhaps it could be argued that falling asleep in uncomplicated closeness with Elizabeth qualified, for me, as a Moment of Being, a rare and touching thing, given my experience. But I'm not going to press the point, for I had found, almost immediately upon embarking on the single life, that my insomnia vanished. It was easier to sleep alone than with someone who turned you on while tuning you out. And when a lover was present, manifestly sexual frustration was not. The big surprise was that even after I had known a woman for some weeks, it was expected that most nights when we were together we would make love. Amazing! Not at all what I had imagined, projecting the model of my marriage onto other sexual relationships. Another amazement: even with virtual strangers, women one had perhaps known only for the length of a dinner and one side of an LP in the parlor, one slept in the unabashed nude, would awaken the next morning to the sight of nipples, pubic hair, whatever, on cheerful, indeed quite unthinking, display. Given this more recent history, it was actually rather a novelty to sleep as modestly as Elizabeth and I did that night. I remember drowsily musing that it was appropriate to our surroundings. Claridge's is not some motel, after all. I was even glad that, in these august circumstances, I had remembered to bring my bathrobe.

If there was, for me, a true Moment of Being in these first twenty-four hours, it came the next morning. We awakened early. Or rather Elizabeth did, probably because she was still jet-lagging. The first thing I felt was her hand on me. I started to turn to her, instinct shouldering sleep aside. But she stopped me, and made me lie still. Then earnestly, soberly, in total silence, she began making love to me.

She insisted only on my passivity, and it made me anxious, this surrender she required of me. Despite what she was doing, there was something terribly self-absorbed in her manner, as if she was proving something to herself—or possibly testing herself in some way.

I kept trying to seize the initiative from her. But she was determined that I should not. The whole time she said only one thing to me: "Please . . . I want it this way."

When she was finished, she flung herself back on her pillow, her breathing harsh, her eyes very wide, something shining in them—some exhilaration, some triumph—I could not fully comprehend. I stroked her hair, brushing damp tendrils away from her forehead. I kissed her. She caught the question in my eyes, and lightly touched my cheek. "Ask me no questions, I'll tell you no lies," she said.

So I didn't. I rolled over, reached for my cigarettes, offered her one, which she took. We smoked in silence, busy with our own thoughts. As quickly as possible, I evolved a theory to explain her behavior, a necessity if I was to recover my equilibrium. For a day I had dominated her. My motives, of course, had been of the best. I had wanted to ease her exhaustion and to please her by anticipating her every wish and need. Yet I could see that I had, in a sense, been taking advantage of her travel-weakened condition, of the fact that I was paying her way. Now she was telling me, I guessed, that the fantasy in which we were living was not to be regarded as my exclusive property, that she was not just some actress I had hired to play a role. I might be the producer of this little drama, but she was its co-author and co-director, as entitled as I was to determine its mood and rhythms.

And she was right; simple justice was on her side. And some dreary memories as well. For Marion and I had never traveled well together. She claimed that I was too domineering, so busy asserting my mastery over strange customs and situations that I never consulted her desires, forcing her into a submissive role that made her first sullen, then rebellious, then just plain pissed off. Obviously, Elizabeth had foreseen the possibility of something like this happening between us and had acted decisively to forestall it.

I should be grateful, I thought. And I was. But I was also frightened. I know, I know, it's stupid. We had just acted out the most common of male fantasies, in which an eager and loving woman plays the gentle aggressor, absolving the man of those sexual responsibilities which, let's face it, sometimes turn into onerous burdens. It seemed unlikely that Elizabeth was suggesting a permanent reversal of roles. Why, then, didn't I just relax and enjoy a lovely moment?

I could think of two reasons. One is inexplicable, its beginnings lost in the mists of psychological time. I have always feared loss of conscious self-control. I think that in abandonment there lurks the danger of some terrible betrayal of my secret self.

It's crazy. So far as I know, I'm a perfectly normal fellow. The soul of Jack the Ripper does not skulk about inside me. Whips do not whish through my dreams, nor chains rattle there. The animal kingdom does not gallop through my fancies, and I have never confused the functions of the bathroom with those of the bedroom.

So I don't know what dread secret I fear blurting out, or

more likely dropping a clue to, in ecstatic surrender. Maybe I am just another victim of the Beast in the Jungle syndrome, my secret being that I have no secret, that for all my fancy airs I am, after all, average, ordinary, a boring statistic in permanent residence on the thickest part of the sexual statisticians' bell curve. If so, then it is dismal of me to harbor these fantasies of self-betrayal.

But there was, in those days, the lively shade of my former wife, dear Marion, at my side, and that, too, was an inhibiting presence—and perhaps more explicable. I have implied, perhaps unfairly, that she was a frigid lady, and certainly frequency was not her bag. But sex was not repulsive to her. Nor, when she set her mind to it, did it lack pleasure for her. Quite the opposite. The thing was, she had to be the initiator. We always did it when she wanted to, and in the manner she prescribed, and in these first months away from her my fear of falling back into the destructive patterns of our marriage was overpowering. I had always to be the one who made the first move, who set the pace, who gave pleasure and, in a sense, received it only incidentally. I did not wish, ever again (as I then thought), to be the grateful recipient of the loving gift, to be implicitly in debt to someone who, having the power to give, possessed the obvious obverse power, the power to withhold, therefore the power to punish.

There was clearly nothing soft and dreamy about these postcoital musings. They constituted a Moment of Being, all right, but one in which I was transported for the first time since Elizabeth's arrival out of the present tense into the bleakest landscape of memory—not at all where I wanted to be, intended to be, this morning.

Elizabeth touched my shoulder, and her touch restored me to consciousness of my body. It was tense, almost rigid.

"Don't think about it too much, David," she said. "Don't think about anything too much."

I tried to smile reassuringly, and reached out to return her touch. But she rolled away and into an upright position. She stood, crossed to the window and drew back the draperies. Sunlight streamed in.

"Come on, Koerner. It's a beautiful day. Time to be up and doing." So it was, I gratefully thought.

Fifteen

There's nothing like driving on the wrong side of the road to chase the blues away. It requires all your concentration—and a lot of helpful advice from your companion—to master the business of navigating a motor vehicle down the left side of a highway, remembering to pass to the right, that the easy turn is to the left, the hard one, across traffic at an intersection, to the right. Many hairbreadth escapes, much excited yelling, results. This is especially so if the car-rental agency is across from Victoria Station and you have to fight your way through London's narrow streets before gaining the relative spaciousness of a motorway. If your car lacks automatic transmission, so that you're trying to get the hang of a stick shift after some years' absence, that, naturally, adds to the fun. If, finally, the auto in question is a tiny Renault, on the one hand eminently squashable by a carelessly handled lorry, on the other an eager little machine, straining at its leash, you dare not, even for a moment, permit yourself the luxury of a single brooding thought.

" 'New York Couple Dead in London Crash,' " Elizabeth said, quoting an imaginary headline as I wheeled too rapidly around a Chelsea corner and instinctively pulled to the right —almost head-on into a taxi. I jerked us over to the left, leaving behind me a squeal of brakes and the outraged bleatings of a horn.

" 'Festive Weekend Cut Short by Tragedy,' " I said, adding a subhead to her story.

"Let's do be careful," Elizabeth said. "One of us might survive and the explanations would be extremely tedious."

On the motorway, where the road was wide, the traffic light and the decision-making process slower, I began to get the hang of things and we both relaxed. Elizabeth was navigator, equipped with map and guidebook. We chose the first possible turnoff from the M4, anxious to plunge into the byways, and soon found ourselves crawling happily through the hedgerows on roads too narrow for two cars to pass.

We chatted idly—her kids, my kids, our work—my anxiety of the early morning dissolving in the solvent of the commonplace. Twisting and turning through those narrow roads, Elizabeth keeping a close eye on her map and an alert eye out for the modest signposts that marked each change of course, I felt we were leaving the known world behind. Not that that was in any sense frightening, so comfortable was the scale of this land, these hamlets. It was just that, only a couple of hours from London, we seemed to have found Brigadoon, a place where if time had not stood still, it had perceptibly slowed. The sounds of our world might indeed intrude here (there were television antennas on almost every rooftop), but they would be absorbed, muffled, rendered indistinct, by these soft hills, this lush land greening in the early spring.

"It's like a maze," Elizabeth said as a hard right quickly followed a sharp left.

"Maybe we'll get lost."

"I hope so," she said.

Her image was actually quite precise. Though we did not get lost, the feeling was like that a child experiences in a maze. You can hear the responsible voices of adulthood through the shrubbery walls, you can if you wish call out to them and get an answer. But you don't wish, for the pleasure of being alone,

sheltered by the greenery, but with a comfortably finite problem to solve—how to get from Point A to Point B—is too
delicious. That most terrible of feelings, the sense of being lost
and abandoned, is tasted, but it is controlled by the knowledge
that it has been created by convention, artifice, that one can
break through them and back to reality at any time.

After a while our path seemed to straighten out and then the
country opened up and we found ourselves on a small plain.
On it, at widely separated intervals, huge megaliths stood,
their placement obviously the work of man rather than geo-
logic forces. As the guidebook promised, Avebury stood in
the center of three concentric circles of these stones, and,
again as promised, there was an inn complete with thatched
roof. It served a marvelous cold collation for lunch. The vege-
tables still tasted of the earth that bore them. We spoke of
them, of a noble Wensleydale cheese and a pungent sausage
obviously made close to these licensed premises, of the bread
crust's crunch and the sweetness of the soft butter we glopped
on it—cholesterol being another of those concerns that belonged to the world beyond the motorway.

We emerged into a paling sun, not quite overcast, to stroll
about a churchyard. We paused often to ponder the great
stone circles.

Fighting postprandial drowsiness, we climbed back into the
car to resume our wanderings. We came upon a giant horse
etched in chalk on a hillside near Westbury, and it was fine—
measuring perhaps 150 feet from forelock to fetlock, very
clean-lined in the manner of primitive art, and providing a
good excuse to pull over to the side of the road, stretch and
smoke a cigarette. We moved along to Longleat, and circled
through the game park the Marquess of Bath has caused to
have installed on grounds where once Capability Brown prac-
ticed his art. Monkeys clambered all over our car as we
crawled along, a strange ferocity in their scampering forms
and chattering faces. We thought them weirdly frightening,

much more so than the lions placidly dozing beneath the trees lining our route.

We had planned that Stonehenge, which neither of us had ever visited, would be the climax of the day's touring, and we arrived there in late afternoon, by which time the sky had greatly darkened and a raw wind had risen, whistling across the moors. The car park is across the road from the stones, which are approached through a concrete tunnel beneath the highway. Some adolescents were trying to bully their way past ticket-seller and guard, portable radio blaring. It—and they— jarred our mood and the mood—stark and with a hint of foreboding—that landscape and weather had conspired to create for impressionable tourists. The sense of awe and mystery the scene has engendered in so many escaped us.

Elizabeth marched determinedly about the circle, camera in hand, grabbing snapshots. But when she returned she said, "I hate to seem ungrateful, but it's really much smaller than I thought it would be."

"I know," I said. "*Travel and Leisure* must take all its pictures from a very low angle."

"Still, I'm glad we came."

"Yeah. You can check it off your 'must see' list."

"Let's see . . . that leaves the pyramids, Mount Fuji—"

"Will we ever make Victoria Falls?"

"Why not? Two weeks ago Stonehenge seemed just as far away."

Back in the car, as we eased onto the road, she said: "The trouble is, my time machine just doesn't run backward that far."

"Yeah. Mine cuts out round about George III. It's hard to get very worked up about people who went around painting themselves blue."

"I think it's because they lack literary associations. No Jane Austen among the Celts."

"Not even an *Upstairs, Downstairs* in it."

In the far distance, Elizabeth spotted a spire rising high above the flatlands.

"Oh, look," she said. "It must be Salisbury cathedral."

"What do we know about that?"

She riffled through the guidebook and informed me that it was the tallest spire in the British Isles.

"What do you think? It appears to be on our way. At least not far off."

"I don't know. It's been years since I went cathedral-crawling."

"Let's chance it," I said. I put a little English on the tone of my next sentence: "It's the sort of thing they do rather well over here."

And so we set our course for the spire. It grew more impressive the closer we came, and once we were twisting toward it through the crooked streets of Salisbury, still redolent of centuries past, despite the stoplights and traffic circles, the spire's airy grace, in contrast to the squat buildings clustered around it, became yet more moving.

A great green lawn surrounds the cathedral, and as we crossed the sward, the sun broke through behind us, bathing the stones of the structure in a soft-glowing light, red and yellow in tone. Elizabeth raised her camera to take a picture, then lowered it. "It's stupid," she said. "You can't catch that light on film. I think I'd rather just remember it."

"You'll have to," I said, for even as she spoke, clouds covered the sun again.

We entered the cathedral. And immediately stopped, momentarily stunned by the sound that greeted us as we swung open the heavy side door through which visitors were directed. It was a boys' choir, voices lifted in plainsong.

"Evensong," Elizabeth whispered. It had never occurred to us, irreligious as we were, that the great church might be in use. Cathedrals—as we later discussed—seemed nowadays consecrated only to tourism. It was curious to find the ancient rites proceeding, seemingly untouched by all the blather of the post-Darwinian, post-Marxist, post-Freudian age. Once that would have brought forth from me some Menckenian jibe. Now it touched me. As it obviously did Elizabeth.

The cathedral's nave was extraordinarily long. One could walk quietly about in it, even whisper, without disturbing the handful of worshipers gathered in the shelter of the chancel. The hymn ended as we approached that realm of ornately carved wood and stone, glowing with the light of a hundred candles. Beyond, the altar was bathed in a very gentle electric light. A priest read a short lesson as we drew near. The biblical passage was obscure, and seemed deliberately chosen so as not to intrude some sharp metaphorical point on a ritual designed to comfort rather than to stir. Soon enough, the choir began to sing again.

Still not speaking, we drifted away, pausing to study the memorial tablets affixed to the walls of the nave. The majority of them were sacred to the memory of young men of good family and good regiment who had been wasted a half century earlier on the Somme, that infamous river. Here was history that indeed held a resonance for us, and one wondered: did one of these tablets bear the name of that gallant who led forth from the trenches dribbling a football? How many here were among the thousands who carried *The Oxford Book of English Verse* (Sir Arthur Quiller-Couch, ed.) in their haversacks? How many had left behind in their dugouts those tins and boxes and jars Fortnum & Mason's found it so convenient to ship to the front? How many of these fox-hunting gentlemen had died with their illusions still intact, thanks to the lunatic persistence of these symbols of continuity? How many had died knowing they were not making the world safe for democracy, but merely for modernism and its fashions of absurdity and despair? Would any among them have believed, in the awful summer of 1916, the century's teens, that some part of their immortality would consist of having their names fall under the eyes of an American couple, off on an illicit weekend in the West Country? Would any of them have been comforted to know that their sacrifice had in it the power to move us, to make us think well of their defense, not of a political realm, but of a realm of custom and sensibility whose passing we mourned? After all the passing of this realm and the effect of its loss were in some immeasurable way responsible for the transitions we had lately been forced to make and thus for our presence here.

I did not dwell long on these thoughts. I glanced away from the tablets and my eyes met Elizabeth's. They glistened with some understanding I judged not far different from my own. The thin, unbearably poignant song of the choir, light and piercing—an arrow of sound—curved upward into the cathedral's vaulting and seemed to catch there, never to return to this earth. Wordlessly, we clasped hands, and as the choir filed out, still singing, we left the cathedral.

Sixteen

"Isn't it stupid? I feel embarrassed."

Elizabeth stood irresolute in the kitchen, paring knife in hand, the groceries we had stopped to purchase spread before her on the wood-block counter, a man's canvas apron tied over the blouse and blue jeans into which she had changed as soon as we had arrived and unpacked.

The cottage was perfect, standing at the edge of the village, on a tree-shaded lane, just beyond the small church. It was, we agreed, a microcosm of England—old, sturdy, small, comfortable, an honest structure, a perfect square of bricks, two stories high, furnished with solid antiques one did not feel afraid to make use of.

I was seated at the kitchen table, sipping at one of the two martinis I had made. "Why embarrassed?" I asked.

She hesitated, then, shredding fiercely away at the lettuce for our salad, she said. "It's one thing to go to bed with a lover, quite another to make dinner for him. Come to think of it, I've never done it before."

She switched her attention to the scallions—chop, chop, chop. "Then, of course, there's the whole business of living inside someone else's shell . . . this house."

I got up, stood behind her and slipped my arms around her

waist. "A good question," I said. "Is room service a requisite for romance? Conversely, does domesticity deal it a death blow?"

"Tune in next week for the answers to these and other exciting questions."

"You want me to set the table or break the eggs into a bowl or something?" I asked.

"Well, if you ever want to eat, you're going to have to stop nibbling my ear," Elizabeth said.

And so we set to work on our simple meal: mushroom omelets, a crunchy crusted bread, baked by human hands, a raw red wine, in addition to the salad. There was a country pâté to start and a hunk of Stilton and biscuits to go with the coffee at the end. I think it is the best meal I've ever eaten, a thing of strong, simple, very fresh tastes. Naturally, we ate it by candlelight.

Lingering over the coffee, I said to Elizabeth: "How now? Still feel awkward?"

"It's not quite like frying up a mess of chops for the kiddies, is it?" she said.

"And I'm not even going to mind doing the dishes, the way I used to."

"You're kind of handy around a kitchen, aren't you? I'm surprised."

"Not half as surprised as Marion would be."

"Used to pull the old helpless act, did you?"

"Yeah. I think Marion was kind of counting on that when I first left."

"Meaning?"

"Meaning I'm pretty sure she thought I'd come crawling back, sick of eating out of cans and watching my T-shirts go round and round at the laundromat."

"And how did you avoid this terrible fate?"

"Well, first of all I patronized the Chinaman on the corner. And then I learned to do some simple things in the kitchen. And of course, I eat out a lot."

She laughed. "I did our taxes this year, all by myself. It's nowhere near as hard as Hilton made it out."

"Neither are eggs Benedict."

"Of course, it helps if the income you're paying taxes on is zilch. Do you really think Marion expected you back?"

"Just long enough to tell me to pull up my socks and be a man."

"Bitter."

I got up and started making a pile of the dishes, which I then transported to the sink. I ran hot water over them while I searched out soap and scouring pads and a more precise answer to the charge of bitterness. It was there, obviously, but it appeared as sudden flashes of anger, the distance between them increasing as time passed.

"There's a metaphor that occurred to me, right after I moved out."

"Which was?"

I laughed. "A hairball. You know, a nasty little tangle of emotions, lodged in your gut."

"Very colorful," she said. She was next to me at the sink, wielding a towel.

"Also very helpful. Cats get them by paying too much attention to themselves. Lick, lick, lick all the time."

We finished tidying up and moved into the living room. The air was musty there, slightly damp, the way it always is in houses that are lived in mostly on weekends. I built a fire in the small fireplace. It turned out to draw extraordinarily well. And, as I expected, the wood stacked neatly next to it was perfectly cured; our host would not have tolerated green logs.

There was a stack of oversized pillows, and Elizabeth arranged them before the fire while I poured the cognac into snifters. We lolled before the blaze, permitting it to half hypnotize us. At length Elizabeth spoke:

"What do you think will happen?"

"We'll get sleepy and go to bed."

"I was thinking in somewhat longer terms."

"Why, darling, we'll fall in love and have lots and lots of children. And we'll live in the country and you'll paint and I'll complete my sonnet sequence."

She punched me lightly in the ribs. "And we'll live on nuts and berries and wear sandals."

"Precisely."

"No, really. I don't think I'll ever remarry."

"That's what they all say. But statistics tell us that four out of five of us do."

"It really does seem to me that fifteen or twenty years of it is enough for one lifetime."

"Yeah, but people get scared. I had this discussion with my partner Mort once. We'd just agreed that neither of us should ever get married again. Then he looked up at me, with his eyes literally rolling in panic: 'But what do you do if you get sick? I don't want to end up in the Beth-El Home.'"

"I have this fantasy," Elizabeth said. "There's this little villa at Cap d'Antibes. By that time I'm very old. But very wise. I'm in a wheelchair and dressed all in black. But there's this divine youth pushing it. I think he's a young composer I'm supporting."

"But seriously, folks . . ."

"I know. I could end up on one of those islands in the middle of Broadway, sitting on a bench and feeding the pigeons."

"Surely the truth lies somewhere in between."

"O.K. What's your fantasy?"

"It's more a model I ran into than a fantasy."

I paused, sloshing the brandy around in the snifter the way those Claude Rains types used to in the movies. "It was when I was doing that documentary about the cliff-dwellers in New Mexico a couple of years ago. There was this old movie director, Colley Chambers, living down there. He heard about us and invited us out to his ranch for a drink. Which turned into many drinks and dinner. Anyway, he was married three or four times when he was in the business. Now he just lives out there all by himself. He reads and he writes and he cooks his meals and when he gets fed up there's always a retrospective of his old movies to go to somewhere. Or some film student dropping by to interview him for his thesis."

"It sounds awfully Spartan."

"I guess it's no accident he retired to the desert. It suits him. But he *was* glad to see us."

"Sounds like."

"I went back a couple of times. Finally, I asked him about it, how he managed emotionally, I mean. Though you don't exactly use words like that around Colley Chambers."

"He made all those westerns, didn't he?"

"Yeah. Strong, silent men with a job to do. Anyway, he said there are always women around who think he needs taking care of. Then he said: 'Everybody gets lonesome, Dave. What most people don't realize is that there are worse things.' What he was saying, I think, was that marriage inevitably drowns love in companionship.

"Beyond that, I could see he was very proud of his self-sufficiency. He'd chosen it freely, it hadn't been imposed on him, and whatever troubles it caused, they were less painful than trying to live lovelessly with someone whose chief function was to nurse you through the flu twice a year."

Elizabeth looked at me appraisingly, and I laughed—not nervously, I hope.

"I know. It's a fine, big speech, but I'm not sure I can handle a life like that either. But I'd like to. Then if I do hook up with somebody, we'll both know it's love, not weakness, speaking."

Elizabeth touched my hand. There was a loud snap from the fire, a brief flaring, then a dying down of the flames.

"Women think fires are romantic," Elizabeth said, "but men have to jump up all the time and tend them."

"I can take a hint," I said, and adjusted the logs so the flames trapped beneath the top one could leap forth.

When I turned back to Elizabeth I saw that her eyes were closed. She had stretched her arms above her head and drawn her right knee up. She seemed to be giving herself up to the heat of the fire, the light of which burnished her dark complexion. I dropped to my knees beside her and kissed her closed eyelids. She responded languidly, enfolding me in her arms and her passivity. After a time she again stretched her arms above her head and stretched both legs out wide as well. Then she said: "Would you do as you please with me?"

I removed her clothes with teasing slowness, pausing to admire her with hands and lips. She stopped me only when I tried to take off my own clothes. We had lived so much of the day in various pasts, we were warmed and lit by this primitive fire, and so she wanted, I think, to act in some historical fantasy, in which she was, perhaps, a captive taken in an obscurely motivated war, delivered to a conqueror and under orders to do whatever he bade. I suppose it would have been within my power to inflict pain, to demand abasement, to bring forth into this flickering light my darkest desires. The heat of the fire and the evening's drink had loosed the reins of my mind. It made large, Gothic metaphors out of small murmurs and movements.

But of course, it was all mime. Only the very dull have to actually tie one another up or inflict real pain in scenes like this, or endure real guilt in the aftermath. When it was over, I found her grinning at me.

"I think you did better on that test."

"Compared to this morning, you mean?"

"Yes."

"The truth doubtless lies boringly in the middle."

"Which is why you gotta look in on the Antipodes every now and then."

"They're a nice place to visit," I began.

". . . but I wouldn't want to live there," we chorused.

She stood up, clutching her clothes to her, suddenly shy, a

tangle of sleeves and pants legs depending from the bundle she pressed to her bosom—a frail defense for modesty.

"This is all just too healthy-minded to succeed," she said, heading for the stairs and the bedroom above.

Seventeen

We made only one more fire—on our last night in the cottage—and that mainly for sentimental reasons, for overnight spring had arrived, a succession of warm days and light airs. Elizabeth turned out to be an early riser, and on the first morning she discovered that the village shopkeepers were, too. It became her habit to slip out of the house around seven and do the day's marketing, picking up all the London morning papers on her way back. Usually it was kitchen clatter and the smell of percolating coffee that awakened me, and I discovered that Elizabeth was a believer in the big breakfast—when she had the time to make one, as she quickly pointed out. One morning she bought kippers; on another Irish oatmeal steamed endlessly in the double boiler, while we steamed quietly awaiting its arrival at the edible stage. I offered to join her on her walk and in the preparation of food, but she liked having the time to herself, she said, and brief as it was, she claimed it was more than she had had alone—what with her job and her new status as a single parent—since she and Hilton had separated.

After breakfast we slipped warily into the day, like bathers testing the chill factor in strange waters. It was not that we were afraid of anything, for there was nothing to fear in this gentle landscape. Rather we were at pains to be kind with one another, thoughtful. Neither of us had been alone with an adult of the opposite sex for more than a few hours at a time since our marriages had ended, and so felt a need to proceed cautiously with the now unfamiliar business of togetherness.

As we washed up in the kitchen, emptied ashtrays, made beds, checked on the crocuses budding in the garden behind the house, we studied one another's moods before arriving at our plans for the day. Mostly, I should say, neither of us wanted to be hustled, to make a schedule. We needed a destination, someplace to aim toward at some point in each day, but we wanted to drift up on that point in our own good time, and to feel that if something as interesting came into our ken we could guiltlessly abandon Plan A for Plan B. By ten-thirty or eleven, one or the other of us would get out the picnic basket, and as we made salad and sandwiches and chose a suitable wine, our deliberations would usually have reached some tentative conclusion.

That basket, as much as anything, determined the tenor of our days. It was a huge wicker thing, wonderfully fitted out with china plates and cups that nested into one another. Leather loops held cutlery and utensils in place and there was room enough in it for a handsome white cloth to spread on whatever ground we chose to dine upon. The hamper was so grand, so redolent of Edwardian ease, that when Elizabeth discovered it on her first morning's foray into the supply closet, we felt we had to put it to use immediately. That proved to be so pleasant that it was natural to keep building our days around its employment.

On the first of them, we were not terribly venturesome. There was a castle ruin—a Norman keep, actually—less than twenty miles distant, and the picture in our guidebook had an irresistibly romantic tone about it. An aged retainer of the National Trust manned a wooden booth at the bottom of the hill that was surmounted by the tumble-down turrets and battlements of the ancient fortification. There he collected 10 p.

apiece from us, dispensed the customary English speculations on the state of the weather, and sold us a modest pamphlet describing the uncommonly quiet history of the place—only one proper siege. He eyed in turn our picnic basket, a sign that forbade picnics, and our obviously responsible presences, and kindly let us pass. We dutifully clambered about the ruin, the views of the rolling hills all around. No wonder the place had been so rarely assaulted; it would require a brave and foolish captain to attack such an easily defended site.

The lawns surrounding the structure were carefully manicured in the English manner and, warmed by a westering sun, we spread blanket and lunch on one corner of this carpet. There we sprawled, growing drowsy from the sun and the wine, lazily talking the afternoon away. When school recessed, some boys, neat in blue blazers and gray slacks, came to exercise their warriors' imaginations on the battlements, but they did so politely and with due regard for their privacy and ours. Other than that, we were entirely alone.

I can't reconstruct this conversation, or most of the others that followed on subsequent days. We ranged over our more distant pasts, discovering certain similarities in them, despite our social disparities. Private schools, tea dances, summers at Black Point—of these I knew nothing. No more did Elizabeth understand small-town public high schools, sock hops, or vacations consisting of a week at the Wisconsin Dells. In her family, her father had been the powerful one—a physician questing upward, marrying not just a good family but the contacts he required in order to attain the right hospital staffs, a proper practice, appointments, finally, to various national commissions and foundation boards. Her mother became, she said, a serene tippler, secure in the knowledge that this weakness, tactfully managed, could not be detected in a woman who carried herself so handsomely, did so many good works and all her life dressed in sensible, self-effacing suits from Peck & Peck. My own situation had been just the opposite: a restless mother, unsatisfied by the life her amiable and inarticulate husband could provide as the lumber dealer in a town of 4,200 souls. He had spent his life apologizing for himself, trying to buy peace with gifts and indulgences, and never being able to provide enough of them to entirely still her clamor.

Needless to say, when we married we had only these poor models to guide us, these ineptly balanced "families of origin" —an inelegant phrase I had learned at my psychiatrist's knee, and at which Elizabeth snorted contemptuously. And so this quick, bold woman had aped her mother, submerging not merely her ambitions but her intelligence to that of her husband, who was erratic in his application of the former and, as I kept trying to tell her, was never regarded by their friends as her equal in the latter respect. As for me, Dynamic Dave, the hard-charging electronic journalist, became, at home, mild-mannered Clark Kent, trying to cope with his wife's ill-defined plans for self-realization—which naturally included a complete remodeling of old Clark—just as Daddy used to do. That is, by conceding all criticism to be correct, promising improvement, and buying whatever she felt she needed to compensate for my other inadequacies—which ranged from yoga lessons when she was trying to accept me, to karate lessons when, apparently, she felt she might have to teach me a thing or two.

Of course, both Elizabeth and I had found our compensations. I flung myself ever more headlong into my career, into a world where it was widely understood that, if nothing else, I had balls. Elizabeth flung herself nowhere; she slid discreetly into a series of affairs in which the domestic virtues she was always being complimented on were irrelevant and the wit and intelligence which no one seemed to notice could at least be applied to the problem of keeping secrets secret. And her lovers, she said, never thought of her as "Good Old Libby."

In short, her ability to attract romance functioned for her as my ability to attract jobs did for me: as objective proof that we were esteemed, as confirmation that our more optimistic self-evaluations were not as far off the mark as our spouses seemed to think they were.

I remember being surprised at her confession of unfaithfulness. Not shocked; surprised. She just hadn't seemed the type. "I'm not," she said simply.

There was no bitterness in her tone; there was no bitterness, really, in any of our conversations during those West Country days. Release from that tone may have been the most significant gift of that springtime. This was not something we consciously worked at; it was merely impossible to maintain so far from home, in a landscape so unevocative of past associations.

Indeed, we spoke to that very point the next day. We were in Hardy country. Neither of us was terribly familiar with his work, but Elizabeth seemed to recall *The Mayor of Casterbridge* from a college course and I had once passed part of a school vacation in company with *Jude the Obscure,* but we confessed to a vague liking for those fate-haunted books, a regard for them rather higher than we were supposed to hold according to contemporary standards in the literary community. So we acquired a map on which the locales of Hardy's life and his Wessex fictions were noted and spent the afternoon touring from one to the next—the cottage where he was born, a school where he had taught, a museum where his study was lovingly recreated, the graveyard where he is buried in no great splendor. It was all just an excuse for allowing our little car to gnaw great hunks out of that sweet countryside.

Around four, we found a tea shop—a small stone building, with leaded-pane windows displaying a spectacular collection of pastries—as we crawled down the main street of a village whose name we had not noted, and we decided to stop. The food was marvelous—even the scones had a lightness I had never experienced in a bakery form I always imagined you had to be born English to appreciate—and we lingered awhile amidst the chintz and doilies. When Elizabeth asked for another pot of tea, I warned:

"You'd better drink it fast. We could miss the grave if it gets much darker."

She laughed. "That's one thing I never imagined about you."

"What?"

"Your devotion to tourism."

"One of the few forms of self-improvement that can't possibly do any harm to anyone else."

"Perish the thought."

She looked at me appraisingly. "You are the most pathologically independent man! Do you have to see everything for yourself? Don't you ever take anyone's word for anything?"

"Reporter's instinct. I do like to go over the ground myself." I paused, then added: "Unless, of course, you make me drink my tea too fast."

"In college it began to dawn on me that I'm not educable as part of a group. Everything that's ever really stuck with me I've learned alone, or going one on one with somebody or something—a book or a picture, whatever. Then, when the marriage started to go bad, I discovered I couldn't deal with *that* in a crowd either. The missis—she could. She really loved group shrink. It was an extension of dance class by other means."

"What bugged you?"

"Mostly, the dialogue. All that 'I can relate to your pain' shit. Not to mention the general air of earnest piety, the smugness of the newly converted. I quit in a month."

Elizabeth looked at me as if she would be happy to change the subject, but suddenly I found I was incapable of so doing. There it was—that familiar flash of remembered rage whiting out the landscape around me. My voice rose.

"It was a rip-off. See, my assumption was that marriage itself was a value, something we were all supposed to believe in preserving. Not so. They were all there to save their precious individual asses. No, that's wrong. To realize the wondrous potential that was being stunted in marriage."

"We're drifting away from old Tom Hardy."

I knew. But I couldn't stop. "Don't you see. Not one person there had a legitimate gripe. They just for chrissake didn't feel as good as they thought they should."

"Now, David—"

"Shit. It's a wonder I didn't end up on a pilgrimage to the Maharishi. Or squirming around on a folding chair in a hotel ballroom while some est fanatic harangued me. Or getting Rolfed, whatever that entails. As if—"

"Please, David."

"As if some half-educated, half-baked—"

"David, for godsake! Shut up!"

I took a slurp of tea, by now cold. I sulked. I lit a cigarette. I apologized. And I added:

"All I meant to say was that you never realize you've realized yourself until after the fact. Even then it's only some part of yourself."

"Yes, I know."

"The other day. In the cathedral . . ."

"Yes, I know," she said again.

There was a strain between us as we set off for the day's final destination, a beat or two of silence between statement or question and rejoinder, as we tried to digest the implications of my loss of cool. It was the first time I had shown Elizabeth hot emotion, and though she obviously knew I was capable of it, she would obviously have appreciated better control. Surely, I thought she had a right to expect me to keep it buried this week.

But later, having soberly inspected our churchyard, we sat down on the stone wall surrounding it to watch the sun set over the hills rolling off to the west. In the middle distance, some farm children were herding cattle home from the pasture as a twilight haze softened the edges of everything, turning the entire scene into a sort of nineteenth-century genre painting. Silently, she took my hand and kissed it. "It's all right, David," she said. "We're one-all in outbursts—counting mine at the Ritz the other day."

I laughed. "I'd forgotten about that."

She rested her head on my shoulder and I slipped my arm around her waist.

"What's past is never quite past," she said after a time. "You can't banish it just by telling the film editor no more flashbacks."

"Yes," I said, and then we kissed. And then, without a word, but still clinging to each other, we were stumbling urgently toward our car.

On the way home we did not speak a word. We just kept reaching for one another, moaning in mock pain. By the time we pulled up before our front door, each of us had unbuttoned all nonessential buttons and we dashed into the house, car doors unslammed, laughing and shouting in anticipation.

So these days passed—and it will have been noted that that earnest inner dialogue, that constant examination of feelings and motives and anxieties on which the author has so frequently dwelt in the earlier pages, has suddenly been stilled. With the exception just recounted, none of that intruded upon us. We talked, each of us, of many private matters, but we were able to do so with enormous openness and thoroughness —the doors and windows of our minds flung open, the dust flying, the junk piling up on the curb. And because our spring cleaning was so exhaustive, there were no nagging guilts about the back closet we never quite got to, the drawer that remained untouched. We emptied everything and tidied everything and each night slept the sleep, not perhaps of the just, but of honest workmen. In short, there was nothing left to brood about, because we had no secrets from each other.

How free we were! Free in conversation, free with our feelings, free with our bodies. We said what we wanted and we made love when we wanted to and, as a result, we were in an unthinking, therefore mildly euphoric, state nearly all the time. We entered into that countryside as uninhibited children, dwelling on the insignificant when that pleased us and hurrying past the significant when that seemed the thing to do.

One day we drove to Bath. "Be sure you approach it from the south," a pretentious friend of mine had once told me, going one up on me with the phrase, and so, laughingly, we did, and then we stopped laughing, for you come upon the city suddenly—round a curve in the road and there it is, spread out entrancingly below you, buildings of cream-colored stone, climbing up from the banks of the Avon on the hills opposite, glowing with an antique patina in the pale sunlight. "Remind me to tell people to approach Bath from the south," Elizabeth said. "Doubtless you'll find a nice way to put it," I said.

We toured the town, sharing an unspoken compulsion to walk the entire length of that architectural marvel, the Royal Crescent, after which we repaired to the ancient stone bridge, and from the balcony behind watched a couple practicing with their kayaks in the rapids below. Elizabeth broke the silence we had maintained for some moments, by saying: "I have a terrible confession to make."

"Yes?"

"Back there at the Crescent . . . I found myself thinking, I wish Hilton were here. Once or twice we talked about going to Bath, but—"

I kissed her, suddenly and hard. "Oh, Elizabeth," I said, "I really do love you."

"What . . . ?"

"I was thinking the same thing. About Marion. I guess we had the same conversation."

"I felt disloyal."

"So did I."

"I suppose it would be a larger disloyalty not to admit it."

"A disloyalty to the past, you mean."

"Yes. And to one's self."

She was right. I told her about a letter I had received from an older friend of mine, commiserating on the news of my separation. He had himself gone through a divorce when he was in his forties, and he wanted to remind me that the process of divorce does eventually end, though he knew I wouldn't believe him at the moment. The real trouble, he said, was that the ugliness of this wrangle has a way of abiding, blotting out the good memories of the preceding years. An irony. A year, at most two, canceling out a third of a lifetime. He said it was stupid to let that happen. Elizabeth and I resolved that we would try very hard not to let it. I hope she's doing better on that resolution than I am.

On our way home, Elizabeth said: "I hope nothing happens to *this* memory. I'd like to keep it intact."

"Wouldn't it be nice if you could put them away in a box, and when you were blue or lonesome you could say: 'I think I'll take out Bath and look at it,' and it'd all be there?"

"You'd have to find some way of preserving it all—the smells, the sound of the river rushing."

And so we came to our last day in the country. We drove down to the sea, to Lyme Regis, a small resort, nestling in a snug harbor at the base of steep cliffs. It is a town of rough stone houses and shops, lacking the commercialized amusements of larger competitors like Brighton. A long quay, surmounted by a sea wall some twelve feet high, and wide enough for two people to walk abreast on it, runs far out to sea before making a sharp left turn to shelter the harbor. Fishermen's shacks are built along it and in its lee the fishing boats dock to unload their cargoes. There are not many pleasure craft in Lyme Regis, and one imagines its attitude toward holiday-seekers is one of flinty tolerance rather than openhandedness. People still work and risk here in a hard, old-fashioned way, or so it looked to us.

After we walked the quay, we walked the beach, which was sandier than most English beaches. We waded in the freezing ocean, found some flat stones to skim, ultimately found a narrow path up the cliffside. At the top, the wind was light, and the grass behind us was tall enough to hide us when we sat down at cliff's edge. A few gulls wheeled above us. Such

133

privacy, such spaciousness. We felt rich and therefore languorous.

After lunch Elizabeth said, "To think—the same ocean that touches this shore touches our shore. It's the first time all week I've remembered that I have this other life back there."

"Our shore? It's funny. I don't think of myself as having a shore—not since we stopped going to the Vineyard. I don't really count Jones Beach."

"Who does?"

"I don't know. A friend of mine once had a vision at Jones Beach."

"Impossible."

"Really. That's where it was vouchsafed to her that her first marriage was definitely over."

"It's the trash cans stretching to infinity in neat municipal rows. Very depressing."

"Actually, it was the Coke. She and her husband got into this terrible fight over whether a second one would irreparably rot their daughter's teeth."

"What about you?" Elizabeth asked. "When did you know?"

"When for no reason at all she refused to go to a Christmas party we had always gone to—a *good* Christmas party. You?"

"The third morning in a row he slept late and I had to move his goddam car from one side of the street to the other so he wouldn't get a parking ticket."

A silence fell between us as we considered the banality of the signals that presaged changes of such large consequence.

"On the whole, I think I'd prefer a straightforward, even melodramatic statement," I said.

"Yes," she said. "That's another deal we could make."

"I didn't have anything immediate in mind," I said quickly.

"Nor I. Still . . ."

"Still."

Out on the ocean, now beginning to be backlit by the sun, some fishing boats were chugging toward the harbor, making slow progress against a tide which had just started to change.

"I love you, Elizabeth," I said, keeping my eyes fixed on the little boats.

She did not reply. Finally, I turned to her. She caught my glance and held it.

"I want to say it," she said. "I just think I shouldn't."

"Just this minute? Just this week?"

"Yes. All right. Just this minute. Just this week. Very much."

"Thank you," I said foolishly.

"Don't be silly," she said.

"You're right," I said. "It was the 'very much' that got me."

"Oh, David," she said. "It's the whole damned week that's got me."

"It was supposed to. But there aren't any strings attached, you know. Except for the odd, kind thought in your wheelchair at Cap d'Antibes."

She reached for the wine bottle, poured the little bit remaining in it into our empty glasses, raised hers and toasted: "To a lack of strings."

"May we not live to exchange head colds," I responded.

After which, we lay together, hidden by the grass, and made love. I loved seeing her body by sunlight. I loved the warmth of that sun on my flesh. Most of all, I loved my new-found shamelessness.

Eighteen

There, on that wild and windy shore, locked in loving embrace, the world well lost, themselves well found, the sensible narrator would leave his protagonists, in the process leaving his readers with a certain ambiguous hope. In an artful scheme of things, the onlooker would be encouraged to believe that perhaps David and Elizabeth—such nice people, after all— would, despite their doubts, despite their cursed self-consciousness, Work Things Out. That is to say, learn how to sustain their love in the real world, where head colds, alas, occur and the basement pipes burst on Sundays, and the one unavoidable topic for lovers is, finally, vaginitis.

But the truth will out. Time out of time is the one sort of time that has to stop. There are penalties if you do not use the return portion of your excursion-rate airline ticket when you said you would, penalties if you do not turn your script in on or before the deadline day, penalties—less formal, but no less exacting—for failure to meet your implicit obligations to waiting children and wondering friends. And so the mists began to form around our personal Brigadoon that afternoon, each of us, against our wills, beginning to live in the immediate future, minds turning speculatively to the What Nexts?—my TV taping, the problems her children would present to her as she walked through her front door. And our lawyers—what of them? Would they have made some progress toward the separation agreements we both wanted? And then, of course, there were our exes. What new delights would they have dreamed up for us? What costly catastrophe that only my checkbook could cure would have victimized Marion? What painful negligence—for such, apparently, was his wont—would Hilton have inflicted upon his kids? Try as we might to keep our last hours together free of these naggings, we could not entirely banish them.

Neither could we free ourselves from a vacation's-end kind of sadness. There could be no doubt that we would see each other again—in a matter of a couple of weeks. The assumption of continuity had grown up unspoken between us as we talked of plays we would like to see, weekend retreats we had always meant to try. But bravely as we chattered about these, it was clear that what had grown between us this week, this loving friendship, could not be entirely rekindled, recreated on a "date", or even over a weekend—not while fighting the Friday-afternoon traffic leaving the city. We might someday share something as good in its way, but it would never be quite like this, for never again would we be as safe from intrusion as we were in this odd corner of the world, nor would we ever again be as innocent of one another, so open to the delight of discovering how much we shared in the way of preferences and prejudices, habits and hatreds. After this, we both knew we would begin to discover what we *didn't* share, and a lot of our surprises would be unpleasant ones.

But there was yet one more surprise left for me on this last day. And there was nothing unpleasant about it. It was after dinner. We had finished with the washing up and I had stepped outside to look at the stars, to be alone for a moment in order to calm the anxiety I was feeling over leaving this house and stepping back into the world. I wanted to preserve, to the very end, the calmness that had been between us. Neither of us needed, just then, any more high emotional dramas.

Divorce provides—for a year and more, perhaps for a lifetime —all anyone requires in that regard. And so I breathed deeply, reflected on the stars in their courses, generally collected myself.

Then I heard a tapping on a window. I looked up and saw Elizabeth standing in our bedroom window. She raised the sash and said, "Can you come up for a minute? I need you." "Sure," I said, and turned to the door.

When I reached the room, I found that she had lit it with many candles, collected from all over the house. She was wearing her robe, tied very loosely, and when I started to speak she gestured for silence and began unbuttoning my shirt. I helped her with it, and shrugged quickly out of the rest of my clothes. She led me to the bed, and once we had stretched out on top of it, it was made clear to me that I was expected to continue to follow where she led.

It was our first morning in London all over again—but how different this time. For what had grown up between us in the days since, especially on my part, was trust. I had lived many years in an economy of scarcity, in which, because sexual encounters were so rare, one tended to attach enormous significance to them, to approach them with caution (since any mistake could tarnish the experience, if not cause it to evaporate entirely), to proceed with circumspection (lest coitus interruptus of a kind not discussed in marriage manuals occur), and to brood long about them in the aftermath, wondering if one had incurred some debt for which demand for payment might suddenly be presented, given some offense for which, inevitably, some retribution would be exacted. And, needless to say, there were certain taboos that were never to be violated.

Now, though, Elizabeth and I had been together these many days, and it had been made clear to me that she was not a sexual bookkeeper, totaling up our transactions in some mental ledger, that she was moved, always, by the inspiration of the moment and looked back neither in anger nor in sorrow on anything that occurred between us. Awkwardnesses were laughed off, confusions expected and not condemned, pleasures given and taken not in hopes of precisely calculated repayments, but with confidence that over the long, trusting run, pleasure would be returned with pleasure.

I think I might never have learned this very simple thing about sex had we not had this week together, would never have learned how to accept love as a gift, not an obligation, would never have learned to accept a woman as a full partner, free to contribute whatever she liked to the sexual partnership, to lead it when she liked, and in the leading not threaten my manhood but enhance it.

Derisive snickers from the feminists? Fine, you're entitled. A similar response from men cleverer in the ways of love than I was? O.K. with me. I may have been a slow learner, but my ignorance was not invincible, and this night there were no inhibitions between us, no mental reservations. She used my body in whatever manner occurred to her, and I used her similarly. Everything was open, shamelessly so, to our eyes, our mouths, our hands. We rested occasionally, but we never slept, not entirely. One by one the candles guttered out and finally daylight began to appear. Each time we joined together I was sure it would be the last time, but then we would rest and talk and one or the other of us would doze off, only to be awakened by the other's kiss or touch. We were committing one another to memory—so I thought—and each time we thought we had the poem down pat it seemed we had to check it out again, make sure we were not misplacing a punctuation mark, making some minor substitution of pronoun or article that would slightly falsify those recitals we knew we would want to make to ourselves of what we had learned by heart this night.

Finally, exhaustion overcame us and the awakening birds sang us to a sleep from which we awoke, sore and groggy, at midmorning. We smiled a lot at each other that day—knowingly, warily, sheepishly, wryly—but affection held. We were back in London a little after noon, and Elizabeth insisted on shopping. "I need the normalcy," she said.

She bought sweaters for her kids, and had them sent, so she could pretend that she had mail-ordered them from a Fortnum's catalog. For herself she bought anonymous things— shoes, a belt, a shirt at Turnbull's, unable to resist the price as compared to the same item at Bonwit's. In Bond Street we split up briefly, each knowing, I'm sure, that we were going to buy each other a commemorative gift, but saying not a word about it.

We exchanged them that night at Giovanni's, which is in Goodwin's Court, an ancient walkway so narrow and dim-lit that we passed it twice before finding the turn-in off St. Martin's Lane. The restaurant was narrow and dim-lit, too, with waiters who somehow managed to be talkative without being intrusive. Elizabeth bantered with them in Italian, and of course we had Sambuca.

What I gave her was a blank book, bound in supple leather by Smythe's. "You said something about starting a diary," I said. "But if that doesn't work out, you can turn it into a sketchbook."

She had bought me a small onyx box, the stone handsomely patterned and cut so thin it was translucent. "If you look inside," she said, "you'll find some of those memories you wanted to store. I hope you'll fill it up someday."

I sniffed at it. "Not Bath. I think it's the sea at Lyme Regis."

"It all depends on your mood."

I looked away, feeling briefly as if I might shed a tear. "You win the best-present present," I said finally.

"No debts and no regrets. I thought that was our deal."

"I keep forgetting."

"Well, don't," she said, taking my hand gently in hers.

Nineteen

Of this part of our story there is little left to tell. We went home to the flat in Knightsbridge—small, a walk-up, rather artfully spare in its décor and furnishings—that had been sublet to me by a documentary director, who was surely even then acquiring more primitive *objects d'art* for his well-lit *étagères* as he slogged through darkest Zaire in search of yet another anthropologically curious tribe. We spent a little time admiring his stuff, talked but little and then retired, put our arms around each other and slept. We did not even make love that night. The next morning, though, we did—slowly, sweetly, pensively. Afterward, I brought Elizabeth breakfast in bed, and then it was time for her to pack.

This we managed slowly, fussily, attending closely to details, thus keeping our emotions at bay. In due course, I called for a cab and in due course it came. We arrived early at the airport and spent an inordinate amount of time at the newsstand, where Elizabeth used up the last of her small English change buying paperbacks and magazines.

"Goodness, I feel entirely untouched by contemporary English culture. Where was all this famous London theater I keep hearing about?"

"I think it's all playing on Broadway right now."

"Since everybody thinks I've been in Tulsa, it really doesn't matter."

"How did you like Tulsa?" I asked.

"Wonderful," she said. "Lots of funny accents, though."

We were almost at the passageway to the international lounge, through which I was not permitted to follow her. People were milling about, torn between their desire to prolong their farewells and their concern over such delays as might be imposed on them by the customs and immigration people lurking on the far side of the partition. We looked at each other and found nothing more to say. We touched hands. "I'm not fond of long farewells," Elizabeth said. "Yeah," I said. She asked me if I thought it proper to write Sir Miles and thank him for his hospitality, even though they hadn't met. I said that was very English of her, the thank-you note being as much a national hobby as queueing. She said that nicely raised Eastern Seaboard ladies were no slouches in that department either. I gave her the address. There was another silence.

Finally, she said, "Gotta go."

"What can I say?" I asked.

"What can *I* say? Thanks for everything?"

I laughed. "Oh, please. That's the last thing my wife said to me the day I moved out. As if it were the end of an awfully nice weekend instead of fifteen years."

"Words do fail us sometimes, don't they? How do you like 'I'll never forget it'?"

"A lot better."

She took my face in her hands and we kissed, clinging hard to one another. No peck-on-the-cheek airport good-bye for us. Let 'em stare.

Finally, we broke. Our eyes met and held. Tears glistened in hers—in mine, too, I imagine. We were searching for a phrase that would put a perfect period to our time together. We couldn't find it.

"Happy landings," I said.

"Ta," she said. And then she was gone, darting quickly

under the "Passengers Only" sign without looking back.

I turned away and discovered as I took my first steps back into ordinary life that my knees were literally weak. In a lifetime of good-byes, in a lifetime of life, this was only the second time it had ever happened to me—both times because of Libby. I thought I might have to find a chair, but I wanted desperately to get out of that terminal, to find some work to bury myself in, so I took several deep breaths, squared my shoulders and quick-marched to the cab rank. Really cool, really smooth, I stumbled on the stairs and, unseeing, bumped into two children and a little old lady, who was very cross with me.

But the sadness disappeared by the time I regained our offices, and I sailed through my last ten days in England with a kind of goony serenity that doubtless made me a faintly comic figure to some of my co-workers, an irritating one to the rest of them. I've known highs in the past, that controlled state of delirium in which, when you write, for example, the absolutely right word, the perfectly felicitous phrase, just seems to appear unbidden on the end of your ballpoint. Tennis players call it being "in the zone," and for them, of course, it means that their first serves always go in and they seem to float easily over to make gets that normally they couldn't lay a racket on. Very often, of course, these moods occur when they are of small value to you—when the writer is doing a book review for some publication no one will ever see, or the tennis player is smashing his way through the draw in Helsinki or Tucson or some other unlikely spot. It's rare that it comes over you when you really need it, but I smoothed out that script of mine most agreeably, and on the studio floor, taping, I was a font of ideas, and endlessly energetic.

It had been a long time since I had felt this way, a very long time. It was not just a matter of the few months since I had left Marion, it was a matter of years, for marriages don't just up and end overnight—they sputter out over a period of wrangling years, in which time you may periodically feel O.K., but you never feel really swell. It's like having a chronic illness, the condition of which you have to check every morning before you step forth into your day, and which makes you move tentatively, testingly all the time, lest you do something to make it flare up anew.

It had naturally been a relief to have that condition cured by separation, and though everyone assured you that your recuperation was proceeding nicely, that you really looked *much* better, certain fears remained. Maybe the damned thing was still dormant in your bloodstream, and all you had to do was get in a run-down condition—that is to say, try to have a "meaningful relationship" with a member of the opposite sex —and it would return, virulent as ever. Or maybe you were a permanent invalid incapable of ever again running for a bus, as it were, advised by medical authority to drink nothing stronger than a glass of wine with dinner if you wanted to live out your allotted span. Now, though, it seemed to me that I had tested myself and I was all right, that I could lead a normal, healthy life. I had given myself fully and someone had given herself fully to me and we were both just fine, thank you: no aftereffects, except nice ones. Do you wonder that I floated, a benign and serene figure, through these days, returning at night to what I had imagined might be a desperately lonely bed, to sleep in it the most restful of sleeps?

On the last day of taping, Miles drew me aside, commented on my obvious state of well-being, and handed me an envelope. "I thought you might like to see this," he said. "Indeed, I rather imagine it's addressed as much to you as to me."

Inside was a note from Elizabeth to him. This is what it said:

Dear Sir Miles:

I'm so sorry that we didn't have a chance to meet when I was in England last week. But I feel as if I know you, as I was David Koerner's companion on his visit to your house in Dorset earlier this week. It is a lovely place, as warm and understated (and civilized) as one of those performances of yours that so many of us cherish. I wanted to thank you for letting us share in the ambiance you have created there. Those days will always have a very special meaning for me.

Dear me, that's an awfully feeble phrase for the feelings I'm enjoying. As I'm sure you know, David and I have had a most difficult year, each in our way trying to come to grips with what everyone agrees is one of life's major traumas. What you graciously provided for us was an opportunity, first of all, to pool our resources and, secondly, to learn together that what had seemed to both of us an ending might actually be a beginning. Neither of us knows what the future holds, of course, whether our paths are now permanently entwined or are fated to diverge. But what we both know now—thanks to you—is that love is something we are capable of, and perhaps less afraid of than we were a couple of weeks ago.

I hope someday we will have a chance to meet so that I can thank you in person for what you did for us. And I thank you, too, for your many other kindnesses to David—he spoke often of you. In the meantime, my most affectionate gratitude.

Sincerely,
Elizabeth Adderley

Miles had turned away from me while I was reading this, speaking to an A.D. about a rapid camera move that made it briefly difficult for him to read the Teleprompter. When he turned back to me, I handed the letter wordlessly to him. I was moved by it, by him, by everything, and didn't entirely trust myself to speak.

"Obviously, an extraordinary woman," he said, waving away the letter. "Why don't you keep the note? I'm most fond of it, but I should imagine . . ."

"Yes. Thank you," I said. "Thank you very much."

And then someone yelled, "Places," and we went on with the taping. It seemed to me to go well, but I couldn't be sure at the time, my mood being what it was and show biz being what it is—with people going around convincing one another that things were swell, that we had a winner here. It is the necessary lie, keeping everyone going while the lighting director takes too much time and the technical director misses shots and the cameramen dolly too slow or too fast. (In the end, some months later, the reviews were kind and the ratings not great, but satisfactory.)

A couple of days after we finished, Miles and I dined together at Wheeler's (the one in Old Compton Street, naturally; actors don't seem to patronize any of the others). Over the brandy, and through his cigar, he said: "I seem to recall, once upon a time, pressing the wisdom of a cautious life."

"I remember some harsh words about improvisation," I replied, smiling.

"Quite—and sound enough, professionally speaking. I thought I might just add that it's often for the birds; in one's personal life, that is."

I laughed. "For the birds? I didn't know you spoke American."

"Only when I wish to absolutely rivet people's attention."

"You've done it."

"I've been thinking of your Elizabeth. None of my business, of course, but there's a spirit about her."

"Yes."

"I have a sense that you ought to act rather boldly with her."

"Oh, I don't know, Miles. . . ."

"Yes, I know. You've both been hurt, need time to, er, get your act together. But I think something rather special happened down there at the cottage. And I think you ought to keep that mood alive. Even at the risk of making something of a fool of yourself."

"But look here. Neither of us is even legally separated yet. We're all friends, including our exes. Our kids even play together—her youngest and my oldest. It's just not on."

"There you go, speaking English. But I know what you mean—a scandalous *frisson* in your circle. The theater's full of them; I've lived amongst them all my life, been involved in a few of them. And on the one or two occasions when I've acted —actually, not acted—out of fear of them, I've lived to regret it."

"Well, sure. But—"

"We're all frightfully egocentric, you know. Just because something is terribly important to us, we think it is to everyone else. But at the most a dozen people will take outraged sides. Most of your friends will have a nice natter and go about their business. And quite a surprising number will be startled to hear about it six months later."

He was right, of course. And what the hell, we'd both come this far. In part because, among other things, after long marriages everyone needs to be incautious, to do something crazy. I said as much.

"Go for it," said Miles.

"It's a good thing I'm leaving tomorrow," I said. "You keep hanging around Yanks, your language will continue to deteriorate and they'll probably take your knighthood away from you."

"Stop changing the subject. Whatever she says, that is not a cautious woman—not at heart. She just wants some support. She's asking for it."

I thought he was right, and having now read her letter to him over a dozen times, I still think he is right. And I've often wished Sir Miles Poynter had been around when the crisis came. Quoting him was not enough—you really had to be fixed by that ferocious eye, coming at you from beneath the famously unkempt brow, to gather the full force of his words, and the shrewdness that motivated them.

A little later, we had a nice wrangle for the check. "Save your money; take Elizabeth someplace on me."

"I shall," I said, "on all the lunches you've provided—and the booze we raided out of the cabinet at the cottage."

147

"Since you put it that way . . ."

"No prob, Bob."

He looked at me dubiously, as if he hadn't heard me correctly. "What?"

"A new Americanism for your collection," I said.

"This time you've gone too far," he growled.

Twenty

Curiosity killed the cat. An idle mind is the devil's workshop. Sexual politics make strange bedfellows. There must be some cliché, some feeble joke to rationalize what follows, smooth it all over somehow. How do you like "the evil of banality"?

I returned to these shores in fine fettle, psychologically speaking, resolved to follow Sir Miles's excellent advice, prepared, if not to sweep Elizabeth off her feet, then at least to sweep away those hesitancies based on propriety that she might yet harbor. If I was to love and lose, let me at least lose honestly, because for some reason that was ours and ours alone, things did not work out permanently between us. The point was that the decision had to be of our own devising, not the creation of some ghostly participatory democracy.

My plan was merely to pass through New York. Mort had begun to screech at me via cable, and my own sense of duty —I resist the term "conscience," as inapplicable to anything having to do with a television producer's activities—was also having its say. So . . . a couple of days in New York to see the children, see Elizabeth, take care of my correspondence, and then on to the West. I was deposited on my doorstep, my good mood frayed by the effects of one of those insane English strikes: a man who drove a fork-lift at Heathrow had sum-marily been declared redundant, thereby causing an unauthor-ized walkout by his fellow unionists, who drove the field's petrol trucks, which in turn forced all aircraft heading west-ward to put in at Shannon to acquire the wherewithal to cross the Atlantic, which caused, in the case of my flight, a four-hour delay on the ground there and made me headachy, distressed in the gut and too out of sorts to do anything but root a left-over Valium out of the medicine chest and go immediately to sleep. From which, thanks to jet lag, I awoke around six the next morning, entirely unrefreshed.

It was a Sunday and I staggered out into a very pleasant spring morning in search of a newspaper and the staff of early-morning life—bagels, cream cheese, orange juice, coffee. Blessed be the H and H bagel bakery on Second Avenue for standing watch over the needs of us singles, its retail department supplying munchies twenty-four hours a day to those members of Saturday's Generation who, upon estab-lishing contact in the singles bars, remember on the way home that there is nothing in the fridge should he/she stay the night through. I even treated myself to a package of the not bad Nova Scotia this estimable establishment purveys, and by the time I had noshed my way through breakfast and the *Times*, I was more or less myself.

At that hour of this day there was only one soul in New York I dared call, my daughter Amy, whose habit it is to chomp and splash through several bowls of Rice Krispies be-fore the rest of the world awakens. She claims she does not actually watch TV test patterns, but she does have an acquaint-ance with a number of media early risers—fundamentalists and faith healers, not to mention antique cartoon creatures—that is more extensive than a careful parent likes to admit.

Sure enough, she answered on the second ring. Chirps of excitement, eager questions, pleas for my immediate pres-ence. A happy deluge. As I had already guessed, there was a request for implementation of the plan to visit Chinatown, and though I feared my poor old legs could not manage it, after the rigors of the trip, I could not deny her.

But I thought I ought to check it out with her sister, who often had strong ideas of her own as to how we should spend our days together, and with their mother, who was known to get pissed off if I did not coordinate my plans with hers, so that she could take advantage of even the minuscule amounts of free child care my visits provided.

"Carrie up yet?" I inquired.

"Are you kidding?" Amy shot back. Her contempt for her sister's preadolescent habit of late rising was withering.

"How about Mom?"

"Not here."

"What means 'not here'?"

"She's having a sleep-over."

"A . . . Oh, yeah. Well, who's sitting on you guys?"

"Nobody."

"Nobody?"

"Mom says we're big enough. And you don't send us enough money."

"Right. Listen, if she turns up, tell her I'll pick you up around noon."

"Come sooner."

"I'll try. But I gotta get my act together."

We said our good-byes and I started fuming. I disagreed with Marion on both major premises. I did, too, send her enough money for sitters. And I didn't think the kids were old enough to stay all night by themselves. On top of which I found myself resenting her borrowing a phrase from their innocent lexicon to describe what might more properly be described as a shack-up. Finally, I wondered—resentfully— over this sudden access of libidinal energy which led her so blithely to abandon her children in order to get laid. In the old days, more than one weekend when we had sought to get off by ourselves, to make love in broad daylight if we felt like it, had been cancelled for lack not of a sitter but of a *suitable* sitter—a hag from one of the agencies not being considered suitable in long relief. But now, for Mr. Wonderful, whoever he might be, no worries, no guilt over abandonment—just bye-bye, and hope nothing goes wrong with the television.

Of course, I resented my own resentment. Should I not be past such pettiness? Could I not whistle a chorus of "Hello, Young Lovers" in honor of the dear departed and her inamorata, in consideration of the fact that, as the man said, "I've had a love of my own"? Odd how these jealousies persist, isn't it? Odd that I could not now resist breaking telephonic silence and calling *chez* Adderley, despite my resolution to wait a day and ring Elizabeth more discreetly at her office.

I reached a bored adolescent, identified myself forthrightly, inquired as to the state of his second-basemanship (I knew him to be the school team's Most Valuable Player) and then asked after his mother. She was away. Oh, really? Just for the weekend. In New Canaan, at the Castlemans'. They were old friends; I remembered them as the ghosts of Christmas parties past. She'd be back tonight. Late. Well, tell her I called. Sure thing.

I broke my dirty laundry down into the proper piles—laundromat, Chinaman, cleaners. I made out some checks. I called my old friend Ellen, and conducted a carefully palsy conversation with her, which she did not entirely buy, she being—flatteringly—still somewhat smitten by me, despite my recent disappearing act. When I finished that conversation, there was nothing to do but riffle the *Times* again. Russell Baker, I discovered, was very funny this morning, but of course, it is his habit to get on and off with exemplary quickness. Finally, there was no excuse not to pick up the children, though even with a detour through the paperback store on Third Avenue, I was hard pressed to stall my arrival until eleven.

The house was chaos. Both kids were still in their robes and nighties, the kitchen sink contained archaeological layers of undone dishes, and there were kid droppings—tented comic books, still-knotted sneakers, ropes of socks—all over the place. After merry greetings and the ritual presentation of presents from abroad (antique jewelry this time: a heart on a chain for Amy; earrings for the recently, pridefully pierced lobes of Carrie), anger flared. Straighten this place up, for godsake, it's a pigsty. There was a great fluttering, and the result was gross improvement. On smaller matters I did not persist. Children simply shed—bits of paper, the odd pencil stub, mysterious plastic and metallic objects—which seem to come into their possession quite unbidden and separate themselves from their carriers in the same unconscious way. As far as I was concerned, Mom could deal with that detritus.

Mom, by the way, had been heard from. As long as I was on duty, she thought she'd stay out a while longer; back at suppertime. I grunted acknowledgment of this intelligence and shooed the kids upstairs, recommending showers and advising comfortable walking shoes for Chinatown. Alone, I brooded. It seemed to me that whatever other changes separation had wrought in her, Marion had become distinctly messier in recent months, and that some of my anger at the kids had been of the displaced variety. In the retrenchment following my removal, the maid had been first to go, but that did not excuse the fine layer of grit one crunched across in these halls, the dust perpetually powdering all tabletops, which were in any case strewn with books, papers, periodicals, mending, correspondence and suchlike. Sometimes I thought it was all set decoration, intended to suggest creative fecundity. Sometimes I thought it was part of a campaign to shame me—demonstrate that all niceties had been abandoned as she struggled to keep her nose above the poverty line. Her standard old-wife's trick of sending the children off to visit me with their toes poking through their sneakers, rents in their jeans, no jackets on cold days, no raincoats on wet ones, surely had something like that effect, and when they appeared so dressed, we often passed the rest of the day shopping for the visibly needed items.

Today, all this depressed me. A certain carelessness about the details of living afflicts all of us during emotional crises as magnitudinous as divorce, but it seemed to me these highly visible manifestations of inner chaos added a particular burden to the children, who, as I've observed, had their own feelings of sudden instability to deal with. Still, so far as I can tell, it is ever thus with separated couples: each sees in whatever the other does proof that those annoying traits which led to the split in the first place continue to persist—gratifying confirmation of the correctness, the superiority, of one's own position. Doubtless the demi-squalor of the house, coming on top of my annoyance over Marion's carelessness regarding proper child care, more than doubled my gloomy outrage, but in all honesty, protestations of concern over the kids' welfare seems to me a tawdry weapon to employ in warfare of the kind in which Marion and I now found ourselves. The truth was that the kids were basically fine—healthy, energetic, untroubled in any large or, so far as I could see, permanent way. So I advised myself to come off it, rose from the couch onto which I had sunk, and went to rally the troops. "Hey, guys, let's go," I shouted merrily up the stairs, and soon enough we were on our way.

Still, I faded in and out on the afternoon's festivities, unable entirely to shake my resentful humor. But my occasionally distracted air did not seem to afflict the children particularly. Their good cheer, their obvious pleasure in the restoration of my company, if only for a day, had its tonic effects. Perhaps too much so, leading me, all unwary, into a conversation I might better have avoided, at least today.

We dined at a basement restaurant that enjoyed a high repute on the kid underground—sizzling rice soup, sweet and sour shrimp, and the place's "special chicken" being the menu that had been passed approvingly from one midget gourmet to the next at school. And I must admit it wasn't bad. Moreover, the place was uncrowded and the help obliging. "It's just like a date," Amy said brightly, breaking open a fortune cookie that advised her always to speak kindly of friends.

"Is this what you do on dates, Pop?" Carrie asked, eying me shrewdly, hoping, I think, for some insights into my amorous techniques.

"Sure. Pretty much."

"What do you do after dinner?"

"Oh, I don't know. Maybe a movie or a play."

"Do you take them back to your place?"

"Carrie," cried Amy, "don't be so nosy."

"Usually the gentleman sees the lady home," I said in my stuffiest manner.

Expectant looks.

"Then he shakes hands at the door, and everybody says they had a swell time, and I say I'll call her next week."

"Oh, come on, Daddy."

"All right, then. They pull me through the door and throw me to the floor and make mad, passionate love to me. And who can blame them, poor dears."

"Daaddy." A choral effect.

"Look, it's silly. Most of the ladies I've taken out have been very nice, and we've had good times together, and that's that. It's interesting, but it's not all *that* interesting."

"Sure, Dad." That was Carrie, cocking an eyebrow, implying she knew better.

"Sure yourself."

Lunch over, we wandered in and out of shops, sniffing the incense and fondling the merchandise. I was several weeks behind on their allowances, and so forked over. There were any number of items they required. Amy, for example, needed a change purse, some pocket puzzles and, oddly, a Chinese newspaper. She said she liked the feel of the thin paper it was printed on. Carrie found a prettily enameled pin, a barrette which rather handsomely held her long blond hair in place, and a kit consisting of ink, brushes and an instruction book on Chinese calligraphy.

All this required considerable comparison shopping and we made almost two complete circuits of the stores before decisions were finally firmed up. Carrie was inside one of the shops, contemplating a rather comical Buddha, which she thought might do nicely on her knickknack shelf, when Amy appeared outside the shop to join me and my forbidden cigarette.

"Is that *really* all you do on dates—go to restaurants and stuff?" she asked.

"Basically."

"Mommy has better dates than you do." Ah, the innocent honesty of childhood. One could throttle it.

"Yeah?"

"Yeah. She got to go on a yacht."

"No kidding. A yacht. I'd encourage that if I were you."

"How come?"

"Well, you have to be rich to own a yacht. And it's in all our interests that Mommy marry well." Do you believe the coolness with which I iced my envy? Or maybe I was even speaking a partial truth. The advantageous remarriage turneth away alimony—a consolation not to be sneezed at.

"Do you think Murray's rich?"

"Murray is the name of the skipper?"

"Yeah."

"Then I don't think he owns a yacht."

"Why not?"

"Because I don't think they allow guys named Murray to own yachts. A Sunfish, maybe." I grinned at her.

"He's kind of yukky." This was Amy's way of demonstrating loyalty.

"Maybe not. You see much of him?"

"No. He hasn't been around for a while."

Carrie interrupted us with the news that she had decided against the Buddha after all, and we began the homeward trek, visions of the yukky Murray dancing in my head. I fancied him an upwardly mobile accountant whose ties were too wide for someone prematurely portly. Or perhaps he was one of those overeducated men who are forced to take over the family shoe business when Dad has a coronary ahead of schedule, thus cutting short his heir's promising career in history or English —"I only had my dissertation to go"—and ensuring his subsequent second career as a disputatious cocktail-party critic of the current best sellers.

I see now that I had allowed myself to drift on to dangerous ground. For myself, not for the children. After the first weeks of separation, as they saw their mother beginning to step out with other men, they naturally became curious about what I was up to and I saw no reason to mislead them, to try to make them think I was some kind of mournful monastic. My tone throughout had been as it was this day—light but forthright —and they seemed to find that acceptable.

No, the trouble was with me. I might make jokes about the hapless Murray, but the fact was that I remained, to some degree, possessive of Marion and, therefore, jealous of Murray . . . of all the Murrays that I sometimes imagined—quite erroneously, I now know—parading through her life. We all want to imagine our former spouses bereft without us, and evidence that they are doing nicely, thank you, on their own is not generally received with good grace and high spirits. I felt, as the subway burrowed homeward, cast down and strangely anxious.

The source of that anxiety was temptation, a temptation to revert to an old, bad habit that I believed, until that moment, I had mastered. Separated from conversation and contact with my children by the roar and rumble of the train, encased in my own wayward imaginings, I was like a semi-reformed drunk fighting a sudden, desperate desire for a drink—just one l'il drink. For the fact was—perhaps is—that I am a natural-born gumshoe, an instinctive snoop. So I discovered, to my high-minded surprise, on my first job, which was as a newspaper reporter. When I found myself taking enormous, prideful pleasure in the exercise of low cunning—tracking down the elusive source, patiently eliciting the damaging quote—I forced myself to quit in order to save me from my own base instincts, to find some way of exercising some more subtle form of intelligence.

But those unpleasant instincts surfaced—another nasty shock—immediately after Marion and I split. When I came to the house to pick up the children, I found I could not resist trying to discover clues about her new life. She was often discreetly absent when I arrived, and the girls would almost as often be dawdling over lunch in the kitchen downstairs, or doing some final primping in their room upstairs, and in these moments I would turn shamus.

It was stupid. I knew she was seeing men, just as she knew I was seeing women, and so what? The details were not only none of my business, but entirely useless to me, maybe even damaging. So the reasonable reader must think. So I now think. But that judgment is *too* reasonable. Remember, there are insurance companies that will cancel your car coverage if they find out you've just been divorced. They know you're not quite yourself in those first few wonderful months. Myself, I think we should all be allowed to cop a temporary-insanity plea for just about anything we do during the first year of separation. You can look it up: all the psychologists tell you that next to the actual death of your spouse, divorce is the most stressful moment in our personal histories. And it's a very long moment.

I rationalize. All right, I rationalize. But I can't begin to recreate for you that weird mixture of detachment and fury that blended erratically in me in those months, can't name all the subsidiary emotions they in turn created. But vengefulness was paramount among them, and so was a self-punishing impulse.

Revenge. She had beaten me to that point where one or the other member of the chronically troubled diad—don't you just love shrink talk?—openly acknowledges that the marriage is over, divorce a necessity, and I, who have always tried to be the packer, not the packee, in life, was furious with shamed anger to be sent packing. What I hated especially was her piety, her steady implication that she was the really mature one, her smug sense that she and she alone had recognized where the greater good lay—for herself, of course, and for the children, and, if I would but recognize it, for myself as well. She was terribly earnest and patient with me, like a third-grade teacher forcing a pupil to stand in the corner, yet at the same time wishing him to understand that in years to come he would wish to thank her for her moral intelligence, for bending the twig in the direction of healthy maturity.

In these circumstances I fantasized getting some goods on her, then filing suit for divorce charging her—Mrs. La-di-da —with adultery. Even if we had had a legal separation, which we didn't, I could, supposing I had evidence, make that stick under the antediluvian divorce statutes of New York, which, like all right-thinking, liberal-minded citizens, I deplored for their Old Testament ferocity on such matters. But what fun it would be—and the possibility was that the court would, in those circumstances, leave her without sou or farthing. Better and better.

Friends on whom I tried out this idea patiently explained to me that I would not, considering the children, pursue my loopy scheme into the public courts, into the reality of tabloid scandal. And of course they were correct, as I silently acknowledged. Still, I wouldn't have minded using such information as I might surreptitiously gather to gain a more advantageous settlement in the privacy of a divorce lawyer's office.

But more lay behind my Philip Marlowe impression than hope of legal advantage, which brings us, on this tour of my psychological sub-basement, to the self-destruct mechanism. If he existed, one wanted simply to know who Mr. Right was, this paragon of male virtues who was one's replacement and superior. Was he wondrously rich or contentedly poor—and either way spared the exigencies of the rat race we who are maddeningly caught in the middle must run? Was he possessed of a steel-trap intellect or was he not an intellectual at all, but rather a creature of enormous sensuality and fine sensibility? Was he a sexual dynamo, a stud sprung to life from the pages of a historical novel created directly for paperback, thus capable of transporting her nightly into realms of sexual glory beyond my clumsy reach? Or was he, perhaps, of exemplary limpness, directing his partner away from the carnal toward a spiritual plane us getters and spenders never attain? In short, who was the sumbitch and what did he have that I did not?

My better self did not want to know the answers to these questions—knew that whatever they were, they could only make me more miserable. But compared to my dark side, which had to know, damn the cost, that sensible fellow, conscientious and self-protective, was in this instance weak, dithering, unassertive. At least at first. He did, however, grow stronger as time wore on and my furtive searchings continued unproductive, yielding up nothing worth the shame I always felt on these occasions. I mean, dare I admit it, there were times when I was so certain that she was seeing a man while I was seeing our children that I extended my researches beyond her study, found myself checking out the bathroom cabinet, where I knew she stored her diaphragm, which was—small plot point here—never out on the job, a fact that somewhat puzzled me.

But anyway, anyway, I managed after a few weeks to bring myself under complete control. For months, her secrets were safe from me, and I could not on that fatal Sunday, nor can I even now, figure out what possessed me to take up the search again, to risk anew that loss of self-respect which inevitably followed these compulsive outbursts. I know, I know—my behavior is not unheard of. If you number even a few divorced persons among your acquaintances, you will have listened to similar confessions before. And there were other factors at work that afternoon as, regaining home, my children bugged out to TV set and homework. Exhaustion, the disorientation jet lag creates, legitimate anger at Marion's apparently casual ways with the children, the open discussion of the excellent Murray, Gentleman Caller and Commodore—all played their part, none really excuses. All I can really say is that, in the end, I got my comeuppance.

Strangely detached, observing myself as I went, I moved quietly to her study. Current correspondence was kept in a small lucite holder on her desk and revealed nothing but deplorable relationships with Con Edison and the phone company, and the fact that her friend Christina, an opera singer of no great distinction, was having another of her fabulous provincial successes, this time as *Carmen* in Dortmund, Germany, if we were to believe her postcard, and we probably shouldn't. Marion's appointment book was similarly bereft of stimulating intelligence. I noted that she was checking in with our old shrink, after an absence—quick backward riffle here—of almost two months. Not feeling so good in the head? Aw. Upcoming was *Chorus Line,* then a hot ticket and not the sort of thing she and I had frequently gone to. Instant vision of pin-striped Wall Street type, flashing teeth, handsomely graying hair, after-theater supper at Café des Artistes, drinks at his place—"Well, just one"—and don't forget your diaphragm tonight, sister.

Still, nothing here that qualified as hard evidence. Last shot: the address book. Actually, it was my old address book, which she had appropriated, but that made it easy to check out, since all new entries were in her hand. Murray? Murray? Murray? Nothing, nothing, nothing.

But wait. Hold! Aha! Here, very faintly, at the end of the *H*'s, was a single letter—*H,* logically enough—and a number. I had always suspected her of suspecting me of snooping—no one with as many "plans" (her genteel code word for dates) as she should have had so blank a diary, recording so dismal a life: very little beyond doctors, ladies' lunches and engagements for the children seemed to occupy her. Clearly, she bore the really interesting stuff in mind, and only in mind, lest I find out the names and numbers of the other players in her game. This light, light marking seemed to confirm the strategy. Honestly! Nobody trusts anybody anymore.

But how easily it might have been missed by the casual observer. Doubtless your inquiring reporter *had* missed it in the past, his eye dimmed by the necessity for furtiveness. Now, though, a feeling of triumph coursing through me, actually grinning, I saw, as I caught my reflection in the antique mirror that hung above the fireplace in this room which had once been my study and lair. I borrowed a pencil and a page of her notepaper, emblazoned with her married-name monogram, jotted the number down, forming the numerals carefully, so I would not later misinterpret them, folded the paper twice and slipped it into my wallet. With the care of the master spy I felt myself to be, I carefully put everything back in its proper place on her desk and then bounded forth, up the stairs to lend Carrie a hand with her math. "Gotcha," I kept saying to myself. "Gotcha."

Twenty-one

"Gotcha," indeed. All I had really ensnared was myself. What, until that morning, I had thought I had found—call it possibility, a wild surmise, anyway a decent hope—I mislaid that afternoon; what I thought I had gratefully lost—call them the routines of survival, those pinched and suspicious habits of mind that are all you feel you may dare in straitened emotional circumstances—these I had rediscovered. Hello, old pals of mine. Good to have you back where you belong. More than that—a great relief, really, after all that emotional high-flying.

So, almost euphorically, I regarded what, had my wits been about me, I should have thought of as nothing but a bad day's work. My diet, now I think about it, betrayed me. For I went home to sip some raw Scotch—why waste the twelve-year-old? —while waiting for the crust on my frozen tuna-noodle casserole to attain that state of golden brownness its container informed me would be my cue to "serve 'n' savor." I am not a cook; I am a heater-upper. It occurs to me that if I had some kitchen skills, if I could have lost myself in the suspenseful craftsmanship of a soufflé, or maybe just a white sauce, I might yet have rescued the day, myself. An assertion of the creative spirit, a touch of prideful elegance, some reminder that the ordinary can almost always be transformed by the application

of a little care, would have been salutary, would have reminded me, perhaps, that if we had not paid attention to
details, Elizabeth and I might have shared nothing more than
a nice week's vacation in England.

But if I had possessed the skill, I doubt if I would have
possessed the will, that night, to exercise it, so busily was my
brain buzzing with investigatory schemes. Here let me insert
a generalization. Enigmatic statistics indicate that something
like four out of five divorced individuals remarry—and in
unseemly haste, most of them. The triumph of optimism over
experience, sneer the cynics. Proof that marriage is the natural
state for reasonable adults, those with a moral stake in the
marital enterprise solemnly advise us. True, true, I say, but
there's more to it than that. We remain in competition with
our former spouses for years, desperate to show them, and all
the gawkers gathered at the scene of the accident, that we are
not such stuff as their bill of particulars was made of, that we
are really swell guys and gals. See how desirable we are? See
how quickly we are snapped up on the open market? To stay
single very long is tacitly to admit not merely that there must
be something wrong with you, but that there always was some
half-hidden flaw that your sometime spouse was the first to
notice and which now renders you unfit for human consumption. For your ex to beat you to the altar is, on the other hand,
a public demonstration that he/she was unappreciated, perhaps blocked in his/her realization of full potential, by the
churl now appropriately rewarded for his/her insensitivity.
One is to imagine the unmarried former mate with nose
pressed to window glass, peering in on the nuptial fete, looking very much like poor Stella Dallas in that great movie scene
(I seem to remember it pouring rain on her grizzled pate).

To change the image: it was too soon, even by contemporary standards, for Marion and me to be pounding around the
track shoulder to shoulder, engaging in this peculiar competition, but not at all too soon for us to be eying one another
warily, sizing up each other's condition, making sure the other

was not gaining some unfair advantage in the starting blocks. Obviously, if I could determine how desirable her potential reward was, therefore how strongly motivated she might be once the gun went off, I would be in a much better position to plan strategy. I think, as well, I unconsciously wanted to begin the race now, this minute, when I had found in Elizabeth an inspiration that would lend strength to my heart and wings to my heels.

Oh, incautious man! Think! Think! What if you discover her in the arms of your superior, someone more successful, more famous, more socially elevated than you? Where is it written that her lover is of the garment district, the insurance agency, the civil service? And if he is not, if he is lean of belly and keen of mind, will you not feel a perfect idiot, and laden with leaden weights as you try to stay your course? Will not all your most dismal imaginings about your own inadequacies be confirmed? And what about your worst fears—namely, that your former wife is infinitely more attractive, more desirable, than you have lately dared admit, that she is far more worthy of admiration and respect (and therefore of the opposite sex's attentiveness) than you will ever be, heavy smoker, heavy eater, heavy thinker?

Naturally, these thoughts strayed through my mind as I ate, as compulsively I did every last dish, cleansed every last surface employed in the preparation and ingestion of my meal. I had not gone completely crackers. But yet I must admit I was in my compulsive tidiness this night rather like the psychopathic criminal who must propitiate the gods with a shower, a careful shoeshine, a neatly knotted tie, before going out to stalk the night streets in search of his victim. I was really more into neatness than into common sense. I brushed caution aside as I brushed aside the crumbs of my meal. My blessed love was, I was convinced, about to be twice blessed. The means for making delicious invidious comparison were now at hand.

Yonder H., who was he? His exchange revealed him an

East Sider, resident not far from me. Thus he must be reasonably prosperous—a professional man of some sort or, more likely, given Marion's tastes, a "creative type": ad man, TV exec, magazine editor. For all I knew, he might be married, which opened all sorts of amusing possibilities for mischief.

But why speculate, I speculated, when so much could be determined by a simple phone call? Answering services, if employed, automatically give out the names as their operators pick up, and people using Phone Mates tend to identify themselves before going into their song and dance about the two beeps and leaving a message thereafter. By calling at an odd hour, one could hope to be rewarded by freebies of this sort.

But suppose H. answered? Why, then, reversion to the tactics of my reporting days would be in order. "What number is this?" you quickly cry, implying that the voice that has just helloed is manifestly alien to you, may not, indeed, belong at the other end of this line at all and may be up to no good. "Is this [insert dialed number here]?" "Yes." "Well, then, is this [insert fictitious name here]?" Nine out of ten times, if your tone is properly peremptory, the confused innocent at the other end splutters forth his own name. At which point faint hearts may apologize and retreat. But the true telephone gamesman presses on, abruptly switching to the apologetic wheedle. One is doing this survey, after all, and if the householder out there has a few minutes. Oh, yes, how nice of you. We just have a few standard questions—occupation, marital status, income range? Do you own your own home, car, boat (Hi there, Murray), etc., etc.? For as long as tongue and imagination and patience hold out—prodigies of the latter usually being forthcoming from the called party, so pleased is he to be part of the great process by which giant corporations democratically determine what lies may best aid them to sell detergents, so delighted is he to have something to talk about at lunch tomorrow.

I actually wrote down the questions for my fake survey, which, taking into account my own professional expertise and my suppositions about the socioeconomic status of my victim, were masterful, I thought; the subject for tonight being public broadcasting, its present effectiveness and its potential for improvement. It's the sort of subject that really draws out your enlightened middlebrow liberal.

By the time my script had been neatly printed out and I had poured a warm cup of coffee and set it handy by the phone, I was in a state of high excitement—the hunter closing on his quarry, and combined with that primitive signal zapping through the nervous system, there was something more. Call it an enhanced state of awareness, something like what one feels when one is about to step out on a stage well prepared and confident, an anticipation of dominating the audience, wowing them. Rich stuff.

I dialed slowly, carefully. The phone was answered in the middle of the second ring. "Yep," said a casual voice.

"Is this 733–8857?"

"Right on."

"Am I speaking to Harold O'Connor?"

"Nope. Sorry." There was something curiously familiar about the voice, despite—or was it because of?—its preference for monosyllables.

"Sorry to trouble you," I pressed on, "but who am I addressing?" I was trying to sound slightly bureaucratic, mildly official.

"Name's Adderley. Hilton Adderley."

I did not slam down the phone. I stared at it. I tried to think of something to say. "Sorry, wrong number," would have done, but I feared speaking even a single word more, for fear of betraying myself. And anyway, what was there to say?

I slid the receiver gently into its cradle—nighty-night, sweetums. The next thing I was aware of was my watch. It told me the time was 11 P.M. Somehow, I lost close to three hours that I cannot account for. Not a thought, not an action, can I recall. There was nothing to show for that time but a disgusting ashtray, piled with bent and twisted cigarettes.

Twenty-two

It was the shock of surprise, not the shock of outrage, that I was dealing with; the latter would come later. As I returned slowly to my senses, a strangely detached fair-mindedness came into play. Given the fact that Mrs. Adderley and Mr. Koerner had, from this great wide wonderful world, sort of more or less chosen each other, they could scarcely blame Mr. Adderley and Mrs. Koerner for making a similar choice, could they? Stranger coincidences had been known to happen.

Indeed, I thought, that was precisely the problem. Suddenly Elizabeth and I, treasuring the singularity of our relationship, were involved in that most tiresome of clichés, the wife-swap. (Unliberated phrase, that—why not husband-swap?) We might as well have been living in some dismal split-level suburbia, where this sort of thing was one of the conventional escape routes from boredom, the subject of sniggers for the sophisticated.

Of course, what had happened between the Koerners and the Adderleys was entirely unplanned. One couple had not vengefully, with knowledge aforethought, responded to the other's affair by hopping hastily into the sack to even things up. There was nothing here but blindness and innocence, and I cursed my determination to violate that innocence.

But that was, perhaps, excessive. The truth will out, especially juicy, gossipy truth of this order. Sooner or later—however discreet we all were—we would all have had a discovery scene to play out. It would have been a shade more pleasant to me if this tacky knowledge I had acquired had been left on my doorstep foundling-style, if I had not been so determined to ferret it out. How rational I was being, of a sudden, how judicious. I was not, for the moment, even curious about the whys and wherefores of Marion and Hilton's affair. There was, I supposed, a certain logic to it. They were both rather frightened people, hiding their shyness, their lack of drive, under arrogant masks. They would not have cut wide swaths through the world in search of sexual adventure. How pleasant for her that the fella around the corner was suddenly available; how easy for him that a suitable partner lived within easy walking distance. One could afford to be slightly comical about them. If it didn't look as if one were doing the same thing.

There was another rub. How would you ever convince the objective observer that this whole business was accidental, coincidental, that there was a quality of passion in the relationship between Elizabeth and me that was surely missing between silly Hilton and grim Marion? How could we convince ourselves?

For this much was certain, this much I knew without having to ask Elizabeth: we could not afford to involve ourselves in a farce, or even in the appearance of a farce. It would spoil everything. And of course, there was no hope of the situation's remaining secret. At least one of the four principals already knew what was going on. The others could not be far behind, if in fact they were not already ahead of him. And after that the crowd, all jostling for a peek and nattering about the comedy on view here. And you would never convince them that the simple, standard explanation of what they were gaping at was wrong, that this was not swap time.

But that was not the main problem. Great loves—even just

plain good ones—are supposed to delight in defying the possibly envious, surely small-minded, commentary of those outside their blessed circle. And I think Elizabeth and I could have managed that. In time. In time. No, the trouble was that the tackiness had arrived too soon, before Elizabeth and I had found the time to weave that protective screen of memories and associations and habits behind which our young love might have taken refuge, grown strong. As it was, this small, fragile, lovely thing had sprung up between us so suddenly, was still so naked and vulnerable. And absurdity was striding the land in hobnailed boots.

I thought we were lost. I knew we were lost, and that pain quite blotted out the other pain, in which somehow ex-wife and sometime close (close to best?) friend had become lovers. At this point I neither knew nor cared whether or not they had cuckolded me in the last days of our marriage, and to this day I don't know for certain, though I rather imagine they did. Certainly it explained why after a couple of years of trying to save the thing, Marion had so suddenly and dramatically given up the enterprise, insisting on my removal forthwith, if possible, to a YMCA. What I had to try, bad as the odds were, feeble as my weapons might be, was to preserve what Elizabeth and I had found. Each day, each week that we could avoid being drawn into this bedroom farce that Marion and Hilton had precipitated would count as a victory, would give whatever Elizabeth and I had a little more strength, a little better chance of survival.

So I would say nothing. I would continue with Elizabeth as if nothing had happened. It was a faint hope, but I resolved that night to nurture it. There would be no midnight call to Elizabeth, no attempt to assuage my panic and despair by sharing them with her. Instead, I took them to bed with me and we three lay together in restless, wakeful sleep. And carefully waited the next morning until the business day was well established in its course before calling her. And spoke in casual cheer: great to be home, how was your trip, the show went well. And felt the falseness wither in the dry pauses before her brief responses. And then asked the question: "You know, don't you?" and heard the whispered answer: "Yes," and felt as if I were falling, falling, falling.

We agreed to meet for dinner that night. But there was no hope in our voices as we rang off, only a touch of common concern. We were like friends of a mutual friend who had died suddenly. We were concerned that the other not be lonely, were anxious to fill the empty space with anecdote—tell where we were when we heard the news, ring up our dismay on a public register so somebody would know that we cared enough to send the very best of sentiments on this too, too sad occasion.

Twenty-three

"When did you find out?"

"Two or three days after I got back. As I say, he was down in Washington, visiting the Winstons. You've met them; he was in the Paris bureau for *Newsweek* and Hilton did a little stringing for him when we lived there."

"Yeah. Sure." Impatiently. I was in no mood for novelistic detail. We were in a fake Irish saloon called O'Casey's, on Third Avenue in the Seventies. There were theatrical photographs and posters on the wall and they wrote the menu on a blackboard. It was like a dozen other places, but the hamburgers were good and the home fries better than that. They had Bass ale on draught. We'd chosen it as you do any place that will do for a working dinner—because it was mutually convenient, likely to be quiet and nobody could think of anything better.

"Well, you know. He had too much to drink and I suppose they were asking him solicitous questions, and he mentioned Marion. That's all."

"And who brought the news from Aix to Ghent?"

"Winston, of course. What Hilton didn't know was that Rob and I had been lovers once. That's when his first wife broke off with him and Hilton broke one of my ribs in a brawl.

Not a nice time for either of us, and we decided to be kind to each other, since no one else seemed to feel like it."

She paused and looked away at a poster for *The Pajama Game*. "Anyway, he didn't call up to gossip. He hadn't heard about our separation, and he just rang to see how I was doing. He really is a nice man, and he was pissed off because Hilton was saying these dumb things about me. So I reassured him, and we chatted about this and that and along the way he inquired if I knew this paragon of feminine virtues named Marion Somebody-or-other."

"How did you respond?"

"Merry trills. Stale news. Boys will be boys." She took a long swallow of beer. "You know, the funny thing was, once somebody said the secret word and the duck fell out of the flies, I realized I should have realized all the time."

I agreed. She listed her ignored clues and I listed mine. Hers included noticing a sudden unreasonable chill when she and Marion chanced upon one another in the course of their neighborhood rounds; her older kids mentioning that for some reason Mrs. Koerner didn't seem to need baby-sitters anymore, an odd silence one time when Marion's name had come up in the course of a conversation with Hilton. "Now I think of it, he looked guilty; he really did." For my part, I had similar shreds of evidence: the odd fact that old friends Marion and Elizabeth, Hilton and I, going through similar experiences at the same time, had not really clubbed together; the absence of any visible interest in our old pals the Adderleys when Marion and I had talked, as separated people so frequently do, about their married friends, trying to figure out which ones each is going to inherit. And then there was the big item—the unmoving diaphragm. How could I have forgotten that Hilton was the first on his block to have a vasectomy when they became all the rage?

"So," I said.

"So," she said.

We each looked deep into our beer, then deep into each

other's eyes, then away. The poster I attentively read advertised Alfred Drake in *Kismet*. It made me feel strange. To the kids trying to pick each other up in here, these mementos seemed antiques, reminders of what they doubtless took to be an era of vanished ease and charm. To me they were contemporary history. It seemed to me just three, four years ago I was rushing about, buying tickets for these hot items.

"I don't suppose it makes any difference. Not really."

"Yes it does."

"Why? No kidding."

"Because I don't want to live in a Grace Metalious novel."

"It's these posters. They do take us back. But nowadays everybody lives in a Grace Metalious novel."

"You know what I mean."

"Can we afford to be so fastidious?"

"Can we afford not to be?"

A waiter minced by—I couldn't help wondering what his fate might have been in a real Irish saloon—and I ordered another round of beers.

"You mean mucking around down on their level—that sort of thing?"

"Yes. Or rather, no. I don't know what their level is. It may be fine and dandy. It's just that I prefer to choose my levels on my own."

"I thought we did." Hurt in my tone.

She touched my hand. "Yes, we did. But don't you see, after this we'd never be sure that we were? There'd always be the possibility that we were reacting. For instance, keeping it going past its time, not for us, but to prove something to them —maybe."

I sighed. How I hate being ruled by circumstances I didn't make.

"We might even do it to prove something to our friends, or our relatives; I don't know. You have to remember, we have this amusing little drama going here now. And the temptation to keep playing the star parts might be overpowering."

"Might . . . might . . . might. How about what we *know?* For certain."

"Which is . . . ?"

"Which is . . ." She had me. If you stepped back from memory, walked carefully around it, studying its pattern critically, it was not a large or complex thing. It was a week in the country, all very nice, but not much more. One might speak of its promise, and I did. One might speak of something even less definable, a sense that we were good with one another in small ways, shared a capacity for easy intimacy, for being good to, and with, each other, which is, I think, rarer and in the long run more precious than sexual compatibility. And I tried to speak of that, too. Finally, I tried some of Miles Poynter's line on her. I told her he had said caution was not her natural mode, that she merely wanted some encouragement to take risks with her heart and that I was the man to do the encouraging.

But she shook her head. "He's right—in general. But he's wrong—for now. I told you that first night. I need time to myself, to figure things out. I thought when I left England that we could do that together, slowly and quietly. But don't you see, David? This puts a pressure on us, on me anyway, that's too much, too soon."

It was my turn to shake my head. I moved some spoons around on the red-checked tablecloth. I had no answer to that. Or rather I had lots of answers, but I didn't think any of them would be persuasive to her. A sad weariness swelled inside me, a weight that pulled my spirits down.

She saw. She said: "There's one other thing."

"What?" My voice was flat.

"What we had—it's ours. As long as it's a secret, it's ours. I don't want anybody else touching it, putting it in their mouths and spitting it out as gossip. Especially I don't want Hilton and Marion doing that."

I looked at her wordlessly. There was so much intensity in her tone.

"You must see—it would cheapen it. No, it would be worse than that." She stopped to search for the right words. "There are so few things that happen to us that are really extraordinary. Maybe we each get five or six of them in a lifetime. I think it's our duty to preserve each of them in their extraordinariness. It's the only acceptable selfishness."

She took my hand again, squeezing it hard. "I want the West Country," she said. "I want it for myself, forever. And I want you to want it the same way. It can change our lives— if we let it, if we treasure it properly."

"Yes," I said. And there was nothing more to say, for I knew she was right.

We sat for a few moments in silence, and then we rose to go. On the street we stood irresolute. We both had a sense that some stronger ending was required. Finally, Elizabeth said: "Take me home with you, please? One last time."

And I did. We lay long together, touching and touching and touching. After we made love the last time, she said: "Do you remember the light on the cathedral?"

"The light you wouldn't photograph?"

"Yes."

"It was such a brief light."

"But it's ours. I'm so glad I didn't take that snapshot. I'll never be tempted to pass it around."

"Or try to explain what it means."

"And how the print doesn't really do it justice."

"Most of all, you don't have to look into all those uncomprehending faces."

"Or watch the colors fade and the edges curl up."

We laughed.

"I'll say it just this once. I love you, Elizabeth. I'll always love you."

"I love you, David. Whatever that means, I love you."

And then she was up and dressing. And I was, too. I escorted her to the street and hailed a cab for her and held her hand until she got in. "I know," I said, "you hate long good-byes."

She kissed me quickly. I slammed the door and turned away in haste.

Twenty-four

Loves—some loves anyway—are forever, but farewells rarely are. I went away and did my work in Los Angeles and when I returned I called Elizabeth and we talked: what I did on my summer vacation. We established the habit of communication, of resorting to one another when one of us had a victory to share or a problem. We became, to put it simply, loving friends.

And for some months we had need of each other. A single mother, raising kids, needs husbandly advice sometimes and ex-husbands have a way of tangling up their kids' problems with those issues that continue to exist between them and their former wives. So, occasionally, I filled in for Hilton on that front. A father, living apart from his kids, seeing them once or twice a week, needs to talk to a woman who has had kids of her own and can help him at least to figure out what questions he should ask in the brief time allotted to him, and Elizabeth was good at that.

But that need faded as, eventually, everyone's emotions cooled. In due course, we were able to group around the lawyers' conferences tables and negotiate our settlements without screaming at each other. These sessions, in time, were reduced to several pages of neatly typed gibberish. Marion surprised me by racing off to the Dominican Republic to get an instant final decree rather than wait the year required for the divorce automatically to become final under New York law. Thereafter, it was no surprise to me that she and Hilton married quietly in the office of an upstate J.P. Amy reported a certain disappointment in the lack of impressive ceremony, but said the small reception, held out of doors on a friend's farm, was O.K. "They had lobster; it was really good," she reported. "And I got to have a whole glass of champagne."

Our house, praise be, had been sold by this time, and I actually had some money in the bank for a change, which permitted me to turn down a couple of jobs I didn't want in order to pursue a program I had been wanting to do for a very long time. I think it's a very good show, the best I've ever done, and combined with the program we did in England, it has given me a renewed sense of professional pride, a sense that I am not forever doomed to the desperate hackery that the last expensive years of marriage—the mortgage, the analyst, Marion's withering contempt—had made me think was my lot in life.

Oh, yes, I have an apartment of my own now, with two bedrooms, and the kids spend, it seems to me, more and more time over here and it is sweet time. When I was married I caught them only on the fly, and usually when I was tired and distracted and, especially in those last years, angry as often as not. "Hi, how are you? Shut up." Now when they are present, I am present—really present and paying attention, all the phones, real and metaphorical, shut off. It is not ideal—I miss the kind of sly, funny, innocently insightful remarks they have a way of glancing off you over the corn flakes in the morning —but neither was our former situation ideal. I'm pretty sure they don't miss seeing Daddy bounce from rage to depression and back again the way he used to.

I live with a lady now, neither of us in any hurry to formalize the arrangement. She is kind and gentle and patient with me, and she encourages me to be the same way with myself, which is more important than she knows. She is as different from Marion as it is possible to be. For one thing, she works at a job, and is entirely self-supporting, which means that she does not have an awful lot of time left over to talk about her need for liberation and self-realization. She has as much of the former as any human being can decently aspire to; and seems to have realized a great many of her ambitions for herself by the simple expedient of finding work that is important and interesting both in her own eyes and in the world's. She is, in short, content with herself, and not the least bit smug about it, which she would be entitled to be, in my opinion.

I suppose because she is content with herself, she is content with me. In almost a year she has never made the slightest attempt to reform me or change me—except occasionally to suggest that I am by no means irredeemably shitty and, perhaps, more worthy of love than I think I am. She says she's known lots of guys who are really much worse and I've come to believe her—almost. She has brown eyes that turn green in some lights. She does not have long legs, which she regards as a serious flaw. So do I, of course, but since, in my experience, they seem to go along with a certain edginess of temperament, I tell her that we must count our blessings. She is learning to play tennis to please me and she brings an earnestness to it that I find terribly touching. One time last summer, when we were on vacation, I watched her taking a lesson with a pro, stroking away trying to improve her poopy backhand. She did not know I was watching, and I'm glad she didn't. The sweat was pouring off her, and the pro was hectoring her in the ineffable manner of his trade, and her tongue was caught between her determined lips as she concentrated. The ferocity of her manner contrasted so vividly with the slightness of her form that I felt something close to a tear welling up in my eye and I forced myself to turn away.

She knows about Elizabeth. I think she is, when she thinks about it, jealous of her. She has a right to be, for we have not ever had what Elizabeth and I had during the time of our time,

180

and we are unlikely to. But, as I've said to her, Elizabeth and I did not have what we now have, and my capacity to contribute to this happiness of ours took root and began to grow because of what happened between Elizabeth and me in the English springtime, when we dared to trust ourselves to love again.

And Elizabeth? The phone calls eventually ceased and we went our separate ways. I saw her for the first time in a long time a couple of months ago. In potentially melodramatic circumstances. The school chorus was giving its annual Christmas concert and had taken over a church for the occasion. As I walked up the steps, I discovered Hilton Adderley standing just outside the entrance. I had not seen him since he and Marion had married. He was having a pre-concert smoke and there was no way to avoid him.

"Hi, Hilton."

"Dave. How are you? What's up?"

"The usual. Making a living, making a life."

"I guess we all are."

"I certainly hope so."

He shot me a hard, appraising look, then said, smoothly, as he imagined: "You must drop in sometime, when you bring the kids home. It's been too long."

"Maybe not quite long enough. But I appreciate the thought."

Marion appeared. "Hilton, I think . . . Oh, David. Hello." Her glance flashed from me to Hilton and back to me. Concern, but not quite consternation.

I touched her arm "Season's greetings, Marion," I said, and passed on into the church. None of my limbs shook, my heart was not making anxious palpitations, all sweat glands were at rest.

The children sang beautifully. Elizabeth's daughter had a solo in the Britten and carried it off with sweet, solemn aplomb. At the intermission, I scuttled hastily for the churchyard, having no desire to be caught in a crush on the steps, very possibly in the company of Hilton and Marion. No sense pressing one's luck.

I had looked around for Elizabeth inside, but there were many pillars and I couldn't see her, though I was certain she was there somewhere. Now a light snow had begun to fall, and as the church was on a side street, the atmosphere was hushed and peaceful. Light streamed through the stained-glass windows and fell in variegated patches on the whitening ground.

I was in shadow, thinking good, faintly sentimental thoughts, when I saw her coming down the steps. She had a suitcase in one hand, a shopping bag in the other. Her coat was open and at the bottom of the steps she stopped to button it. It was awkward, because she did not want to set the bag down on the wet ground. I stepped forward. "Give you a hand, lady?"

"Oh, David. Yes, thank you. I have to catch a plane. But I couldn't miss the solo."

"It was marvelous," I said, and I took the bag while she finished with the coat. She reached for her bundle, but I hung on to it. "Need a cab?" I said.

"Thank you," she said. I hefted her suitcase as well and we set off for the nearest avenue.

"Where you going?"

"Buffalo. Can you believe it?"

"Just barely."

"He's a very old friend, from college. He teaches there. He just suddenly turned up in my life."

"And that is good?"

"And that is good. How about you?"

"Good, too. Very good."

"I'm glad."

A cab was stopped for the light at the corner. I lifted the suitcase and he caught my heavy-handed signal.

"What a lot of good-byes we've said."

I opened the door, slid suitcase and bag across the seat, and stepped aside to let her enter. "Merry Christmas, Elizabeth. And Happy New Year. Happy New *Years.*"

"And to you, David."

She got in. Settled, she suddenly rolled down the window. "David," she said.

"Yes?"

"The light. It's never faded."

The cab started up before I could think of a reply. I still haven't.

Back at the church, the last stragglers were crushing out their cigarettes and moving through the doors for the second half of the concert. The last of the last were Hilton and Marion. He slid his arm around her waist. For the briefest instant her cheek rested against his shoulder. I smiled to myself in the darkness.

Just as my hand touched the door, the music began inside. "Adeste Fidelis."

"Oh, come, all ye faithful, joyful and triumphant . . ." I stood alone in the darkness, in the snow, listening. My smile became a grin, and tears there was no need to hide rolled down my face.

It seemed we were all all right after all.